Lost and Found Lady

By Susana Ellis

Lost and Found Lady

Cover art by Fabiana Gómez Sobradelo; print design by Mari Christie

Print Edition

ISBN-13: 978-0-9908638-8-5

This book is available in e-book format at major online retailers.

For Selene Grace Silver, critique partner extraordinaire and, more importantly, my good friend.

Heartfelt thanks to my long-time friend and devoted cheerleader, Ellen-the-Spanish-teacher. ¡Mil gracias, mi amiga!

Table of Contents

Prologue

September 14, 1793
A beach near Dieppe, France

"I don't like the look of those clouds, *monsieur,*" Tobias McIntosh said in fluent French to the gray-bearded old man in a sailor hat waiting impatiently near the rowboat that was beginning to bob more sharply with each swell of the waves. "Are you sure your vessel can make it safely all the way to Newhaven in these choppy seas?"

The old man waved a hand over the horizon. *"La tempête,* it is not a threat, if we leave *immédiatement. Plus tard…"* He shrugged. *"Je ne sais pas."*

"Please, *mon amour,"* pleaded the small woman wrapped in a hooded gray cloak standing at his side. "Allow me to stay with you. I don't want to go to England. I promise I will be *prudent."*

A strong gust of wind caught her hood and forced it down, revealing her mop of shiny dark locks. Tobias felt like seizing her hand and pulling her away from the ominous waves to a place of safety where she and their unborn child could stay until the senseless *Terreur* was over.

"Justine, *ma chère,* we have discussed this endlessly. There is no place in France safe enough for you if your identity as the daughter of the Comte d'Audet is discovered." He shivered. "I could not bear it if you were to suffer the same fate at the hands of the revolutionaries as your parents did when I failed to save them."

She threw her arms around him, the top of her head barely reaching his chin. "*Non, mon amour,* it was not your fault. You could not have saved them. It was *miraculeux* that you saved *me*. I should have died with them."

She looked up to catch his gaze, her face ashen. "Instead, we met and have had three *merveilleux* months together. If it is my time to die, I wish to die at your side."

Tobias felt like his heart was going to break. His very soul demanded that the two of them remain together and yet… there was a price on both their heads, and the family of the Vicomte Lefebre was waiting for him in Amiens, the revolutionaries expected to reach them before midday. It was a dangerous work he was involved in—rescuing imperiled French nobility from bloodthirsty, vengeful mobs—but he had pledged himself to the cause and honor demanded that he carry on. And besides, there was now someone else to consider.

"The child," he said with more firmness than he felt. "We have our child to consider, now, Justine *ma chère*. The next Earl of Dumfries. He must live to grow up and make his way in the world."

Not to mention the fact that Tobias was human enough to wish to leave a child to mark his legacy in the world—his and Justine's. He felt a heaviness in his heart that he might not live long enough to know this child he and Justine had created together. He could not allow his personal wishes to undermine his conviction. Justine and the child must survive.

Justine's blue eyes filled with tears. "But I cannot! I will die without you, *mon cher mari*. You cannot ask it of me!"

"Justine," he said, pushing away from her to clasp her shoulders and look her directly in the eye. "You are a brave woman, the strongest I have ever known. You have survived many hardships and you can survive this. Take this letter to my brother in London, and he will see to your safety until the time comes that I can join you. My comrades in Newhaven will see that you are properly escorted."

He handed over a letter and a bag of coins. "This should be enough to get you to London."

After she had reluctantly accepted and pocketed the items beneath her cloak, he squeezed her hands.

"Be sure to eat well, *ma chère*. You are so thin and my son must be born healthy."

She gave him a feigned smile. "Our daughter is the one responsible for my sickness in the mornings… I do not believe she wishes me to even *look* at food."

She looked apprehensively at the increasingly angry waves as they tossed the small boat moored rather loosely to a rock on the shore and her hands impulsively went to her stomach.

"Make haste, *monsieur*," the old sailor called as he peered anxiously at the darkening clouds. "We must depart now if we are to escape the storm. Bid your *chère-amie* adieu *maintenant* or wait for another day. I must return to the *bateau*."

"Tobias," she said, her voice shaking.

He wondered if he would ever again hear her say his name with that adorable French inflection that had drawn him from their first meeting.

"Go, Justine. Go to my family and keep our child safe. I promise I will join you soon."

He scooped her up in his arms and carried her toward the dinghy, trying to ignore her tears. The old sailor held the boat as still as he could while Tobias placed her on the seat and kissed her hard before striding back to the shore, each footstep heavier than the last.

He studied the darkening sky as the sailor climbed in the boat. "You are sure it is safe?"

"*La Chasseresse,* she is *très robuste.* A few waves will not topple her, *monsieur.*"

"*Je t'aime, mon amour,*" she said to him plaintively, her chin trembling.

"*Au revoir, ma chère,*" he said, trying to smile, although his vision was blurring from tears.

Will I ever see her again?

He stood watching as the dinghy made its way slowly through the choppy sea to the larger ship anchored in the distance, grief-stricken and unable to concentrate on anything but his pain. When the ship finally sailed off into the horizon, he fell to his knees and prayed as he had never done before for the safety of his beloved. He remained in that position until drops of rain on his face reminded him of the Lefebre family waiting for him in Amiens.

With a deep breath, he rose and made his way to the nearby forest, where his horse waited, tied to a tree.

"Come, my friend. We have a long, wet journey ahead of us."

Setting foot in the stirrup, he swung his leg over the saddle and urged the horse to a gallop, feeling his heart rip into pieces with every step away from his beloved.

~

The rain stopped after a few hours, and as dawn approached, the clouds parted to reveal a brilliant moon in all its glory. Tobias turned his attention to the task at hand, confining his grief to the back of his mind while he went through the details of his part in the rescue of the Lefebres.

His contact in the Department of Public Safety in Paris had relayed the information that the Vicomte Lefebre had been denounced and that he and his family were due to be arrested and conveyed to the Conciergerie in Paris the very next day. It had been a close thing getting his Justine off on the ship they knew would be waiting in Dieppe without jeopardizing the mission. He swallowed as he recalled the image of her misery as the dinghy bounced farther and farther away on the choppy sea.

But she will be safe in England.

There was no safety for her in France, not as a daughter of an aristocrat nor as a member of their company of underground liberators. He could not resist a small smile as he recalled her fierce aversion to being transported to England without him. She could be quite a hothead when she was angry. And she *was* angry. Her parents had been one of the first aristocrats to be denounced by the Department, and after several months of imprisonment, they had been made victims of Madame La Guillotine. Justine had narrowly escaped their fate by hiding in a haystack in the stables, and when Tobias had finally located her—too late to be of any assistance to her parents—she had already been plotting revenge.

"Escape to England? Bah! I have no one there!" she'd argued. "Just let me near that *salaud* Robespierre and I will cut him down with my sword!"

And she could have, had she been allowed anywhere near the man. Tobias had been intrigued to learn that Justine was no spoiled and pampered noblewoman. She could fence like no lady he had ever met. And she could swear as well as any man. When he discovered she shared his interest in Greek and Latin literature, had studied Voltaire and had actually met Benjamin Franklin when he visited her family in Paris, he knew he had found his match.

Scarcely a month after she had joined their band—against his better judgment—and participated in several clandestine rescues, they found a priest in hiding and said their vows to each other in a wee church in the small hours of the morning. Their love was fierce and passionate, and as much as he fought it, he found himself more and more distracted by his fear for her safety. Her pregnancy was the final straw. He could not risk losing her. It was no longer an acceptable risk for her to wield swords, climb walls, and leap out of wagons. In any case, her male clothing would not camouflage her female form once it burgeoned with his child.

The *Chasseresse* regularly—or irregularly—stopped at the beach near Dieppe to take on illicit passengers, and so he'd written letters and made the arrangements for her passage. She'd argued and cried, but she wanted the babe as much as he did, and she couldn't deny that her pregnancy made it impossible to remain with the band. Clearly, there was nowhere safer than Tobias's family across the Channel. If only she managed to make it there.

His body felt cold at the thought of her sailing away from him. It was no wonder the other gentlemen in his company were unmarried with few family ties other than older brothers or a stray parent or two. A man with a family had too much to live for to do this sort of work. He swallowed and tightened his lips together and tried to focus on the mission ahead.

When he reached the outskirts of Amiens, he took a detour past the *Voyageur,* an inn owned by a man sympathetic to their cause. The horse could use a brief rest, along with some hay and oats, and Monsieur Couloir often had news to report.

It was still too early for patrons in the public room or guests to be stirring out of their beds, but the innkeeper ushered him into a private room, calling for his wife, who had already begun the day's baking, to bring in hot coffee and rolls for *le bon soldat.*

"Avez-vous des nouvelles, monsieur? Has anything happened?"

"Our mutual friend tells me the landing at Dieppe has been discovered. There will be another ship *ce soir* for the family of the vicomte, but at Berck instead. Do you know the place?"

He did, but Tobias's heart had frozen at the mention of Dieppe's discovery. He seized the man's shirt with both hands.

"Dieppe has been discovered? How? What has happened to the *Chasseresse?*"

The man's eyes widened. *"Calmez-vous, monsieur.* I am only the courier. We are allies, *souvenez-vous?"*

Tobias released the man and listened in growing horror as he was told that the *Chasseresse* had gone down in the storm not far out of Dieppe, and the French navy had consequently discovered their secret landing site and loaded it with guards.

The room started to spin. It wasn't long before Tobias found himself propped up against the innkeeper who was holding a cup of coffee up to his mouth and urging him to drink it. He took a sip and sputtered.

"The *Chasseresse!* What has happened to it? Are there any survivors? Were they taken by the Republican navy? Tell me, man!"

Monsieur Couloir shook his head. "I'm so sorry, monsieur. I have no knowledge of any survivors. I only know that the landing is discovered and the next group will be collected at Berck after midnight tonight."

He laid a sympathetic hand on Tobias's back. *"Le tempête,* it was bad. *La Chasseresse* had nowhere to wait out the storm. Did you know someone aboard the ship?"

Tobias covered his face with his hands. Could it be true? Had Justine perished with the rest of the passengers in the stormy seas? The very thought was just too ghastly for him to take in.

"It can't be true," he moaned. "It was only a few hours ago I saw her on the ship. She cannot have died, not so soon!" He raised his head and looked hopefully at the innkeeper. "She *can* swim," he said, searching for any sign of hope in the man's expression.

Monsieur Couloir shook his sadly. "Not in those waters. Waves that can sink a boat like the *Chasseresse* would not spare a mere human, not even the strongest of men. My sympathies, *monsieur.*"

Though he yearned to abandon his mission and return to the coast to search for any sign his Justine might have escaped the angry waters, his honor required that he follow through on his commitment to the Lefebres.

It was fortunate that his plan was already inscribed in his mind, because it was more of an automaton than a man who escorted the vicomte and his wife and six children to the landing site at Berck. He stood briefly as they boarded the ship, the faces of the children burning a hole in his frozen heart. He'd saved eight people from the *Le Rasoir national.* He should be feeling that burst of satisfaction that came when a commission was executed successfully.

But all he could think of Justine. If she had perished, their babe would never be born, and his reason for living had vanished along with them.

September 15, 1793
Octeville-sur-mer, France

Soeur Agnès was the first to hear the persistent knocking on the door of the convent. She rose earlier than the others to prepare the bread for baking so that she could attend morning prayers, and she was in the middle of mixing the sticky dough with her hands when the summons came. She was tempted to ignore it, but the nuns had already had several unfortunate *contretemps* with Republican soldiers—who respected religious institutions as little as they did aristocrats—and she knew it was unwise to ignore them.

"Je viens," she muttered as she wiped her hands on her apron, mentally asking forgiveness for her uncharitable thoughts.

But the door, when she opened it, did not reveal the loutish, blue-uniformed soldiers with their tricornered hats and blue, white, and red cockades. Instead, it was a group of villagers that greeted her, carrying a slender young man—no, it was a woman, she realized when she saw the pretty face. A woman dressed as a man? Scandalous. But how very fascinating.

But the young girl's story would not come to light any time soon, because when she awakened later that morning, she could not remember anything, not even her name, no doubt because she had a nasty head wound that gave her pain for many days afterward. The villagers had found her on the rocky beach, so it was first believed that she must have been a survivor of a boating accident and hit her head on a rock as she came ashore.

But as the weeks passed and it became obvious that she was *enceinte,* many nuns began to suspect that she was a fallen woman who had tried to commit the ultimate blasphemy of taking her own life… and that of her unborn child. Since she had not, however, succeeded, Soeur Agnès was of the opinion that *le bon Dieu* had allowed her to survive for a reason, and that she could achieve redemption through a lifetime of service to Him.

And the young girl, whom they called Étoile (Soeur Agnès's idea, refusing to consider *Magdalène* an appropriate name since they didn't really *know* anything about her past), lived with the nuns as she awaited her child's birth. Étoile was happy enough there—she was familiar with the rituals of the True Church and very willing to share in even the most mundane of tasks. But Soeur Agnès knew she often wept with frustration at her inability to remember her identity, or indeed, the identity of the child's father, whether she was married, or how she had landed on the beach at Octeville-sur-mer.

On November 7, however, the shocking news arrived that the Committee for Public Safety had abolished the practice of Christianity in the New Republic. Many of the nuns decided to flee to safety in other countries. Étoile was one of a dozen or so who accompanied Soeur Agnès to a convent in Santiago de Compostela, in Spain. When the time came for the nuns to disperse from that overcrowded location, Soeur Agnès and Étoile were among a handful who were sent to a small convent outside of Salamanca.

And that was where, on April 24, 1794, Étoile gave birth to a daughter, whom she called, for some reason even she didn't know, Catriona. Unfortunately, Étoile would not live to see her daughter grow up, having contracted childbed fever after the birth. Soeur Agnès insisted on seeing her buried on consecrated ground, in spite of the objections of several of the more stern sisters who believed her a fallen woman.

Soeur Agnès desperately wished to keep Étoile's child, but times were hard in that region of Spain, and another mouth to feed was out of the question. Little Catriona was handed over to a childless couple from a small town to the south of Salamanca called Las Torres. Catriona being a foreign name and being thoroughly distrustful of foreigners, they called her Catalina instead.

And, although she prayed for her every day, Soeur Agnès never saw Étoile's child again

Chapter 1

July 22, 1812
Las Torres, Spain

"I think I should like to become a nun, Padre," Catalina opined from her position sprawled on the rug in front of the fireplace.

A gray-bearded, gentle-faced man sitting at a desk nearby removed his spectacles and studied her curiously.

"And why do you say that, my child?"

Catalina tucked a stray lock of dark, wavy hair behind her ear and sighed heavily.

"I have been reading about Sor Juana de la Cruz. She wanted to spend her life studying and writing, but being a woman, she was expected to marry and live a happy domestic life. So she became a nun instead."

The priest's eyes narrowed. "Is that the *only* reason she chose the Church as a vocation, *mi hija*?"

Catalina shrugged. "No, of course not. She was devoutly religious from the age of three. But becoming a nun gave her the freedom to use her intellect in a way she could not had she done as women are expected to do."

She had much in common with the notable Mexican authoress, Catalina realized. Well, one thing, at least. They were both illegitimate, although at least Juana had her mother and grandfather. Catalina had only indifferent adoptive parents who clearly favored the children of their own blood over her. Juana grew up financially secure, while Catalina's family had to eke out a living on whatever money was left over from her father's wages as a gardener after he returned from the neighborhood *taberna*.

Well, on second thought, perhaps it was better *not* to have a father, Catalina thought bitterly. When he was drunk—which was most of the time these days—he was like a raging bull looking for someone to sink his horns into—usually *her,* although occasionally he swung a fist at Abuela, his mother-in-law. For the rest of the family it was mostly verbal abuse, since his wife was both taller and heavier than he was and quite strong enough to protect herself and her own two daughters.

"Is that what you wish for yourself, Catalina? A life of solitude and study? Would you not like to have a home and children of your own? Many women find peace and contentment in their roles as wives and mothers."

Catalina sat up and folded her arms across her chest. "Do they, Padre? I am sorry to say that I have not encountered them. Some men do not even allow their wives and daughters to learn to read and write. Sor Juana wanted to disguise herself as a man to attend university, but her mother did not allow it. Women *still* cannot enroll at universities, more than a hundred years later!

"The mayor's wife is the very picture of rectitude—she will chastise you for the smallest infraction—but everyone knows her husband has a mistress in Salamanca. I do not believe *she* has found much peace and contentment in her marriage."

At the priest's frown, she continued hastily. "Forgive me, Padre, but let us speak frankly. The lives of women in Spain have not changed significantly since the time of Sor Juana. It wasn't fair then, and it isn't now. Can it really be true that it is God's plan for men to mistreat their wives?"

He clasped his hands together and sighed. "Of course not, *mi hija*. In the first book of Peter, it states that women are to submit to their husbands, but husbands are to love their wives as Christ loved the Church." He shook his head sadly. "Unfortunately, that last directive is too often ignored. Not all men are brutes, however."

He rose from his desk and went to stand at the window. "Does this precipitous aspiration to become a Bride of Christ have anything to do with your younger sister's recent marriage?"

Catalina bit her lip. It did, of course, but not in the way the priest was hinting at. She didn't envy her sister's good fortune in attaching a well-to-do merchant's son from Salamanca. Frankly, she could not like the stout, sanctimonious Juan Rodríguez, and she doubted her sister did either. But there was no denying that the marriage had liberated her from the miserable Ordóñez home, and Catalina did envy her for *that*.

"Of course not! Well… perhaps," she confessed, running her hands through her dark curls. "I have eighteen years already, Padre. Clara has seventeen and is already wed, and soon Ana María will be gone as well, and I alone shall be left to suffer Hector's drunken rages."

She never called him Papá. He'd never treated her as a daughter, and he wasn't *really* her father. She'd heard him speak of her as *la bastarda* on multiple occasions, and the only thing he seemed to like about her was her appearance. Since she'd turned thirteen, when he'd begun to leer at her in a manner that made her skin crawl, his wife had found a reason to move her into Abuela's room. But now that Clara was gone, Hector was hinting that Catalina should take over the vacant room.

"Ah, Hector," the priest said as he fingered the wooden cross around his neck. "An unhappy man, to be sure. Consuelo knows how to deal with him. She could protect you, but she does not." He shook his head. "I do not understand why they chose to take you from the nuns at all, so many years ago."

Catalina did. Hector and Consuelo had not conceived in eight years of marriage, and Consuelo thought an abandoned bastard was the best chance she would have to be a mother. For some reason, however, God had chosen to bless her womb almost immediately after, and the small child they had taken in had become an unwelcome burden.

She picked herself up off the floor and waved her hands up in the air. "Surely there is more for me than this, Padre! Do you not think I could better serve God by praying and studying and doing His work?"

"You needn't become a nun to do that, *mi hija.* A Bride of Christ is called to that honor. Do you believe he has issued such a call to *you?*"

Catalina dropped her chin to her chest. "No."

He motioned for her to join him at the window. "Is the garden not beautiful in the summer months? Hermano Pedro toils in the soil many hours each day to remove the *hierba mala* and allow the beauty to flower and thrive. Many a night he has warm rags applied to his back to reduce the pain such physical labor cost him. But no matter the pain, each morning he returns to his labors, and smiles with pride when he sees the pleasure it gives others to look upon the delightful result."

He turned to face her and cupped her shoulders with his hands. "God has a plan for you, Catalina. Your suffering has not been in vain. I sense that He has been preparing you for something quite remarkable. He will reveal it in His own time. Trust in Him and when the time comes, you will have no doubts."

He opened his arms and Catalina went into them, tears prickling her eyes.

"I wish I had your faith, Padre," she sobbed into his chest. "Sometimes I feel God has forgotten me."

"I know, *mi hija*. Only be faithful and the rest will come."

Would it? Catalina had her doubts.

~

A cool breeze signaled the approach of eventide, and Catalina tightened her charcoal gray shawl around her shoulders. Summers were generally quite warm in the area of León where Las Torres lay, but a virtuous young lady never ventured anywhere without being decently cloaked. Abuela had fabricated this shawl for her from an old gown when Consuelo had given her money for a new one (money she "found" by going through Hector's pockets when he was drunk). The fabric was well-worn, but Abuela had embroidered the edges with bright blue flowers that she said were the color of Catalina's startling eyes.

She hoped Hector would not be home by the time she returned to know that she had spent so much time at the church. Consuelo wouldn't make a point of telling him; she didn't care what Catalina did as long as she managed to get her chores done promptly. Catalina felt a twinge of anxiety that she had not mucked out the stables yet, which Hector would realize when he returned. If she hurried, she might be able to avoid provoking another of his angry rages.

As she reached a bend in the road, however, she was stunned to discover a man lying along the side of the road. Not just any man, but a soldier. Dressed in the dreaded blue and red uniform of the French army… the enemy!

She squeezed her eyes shut and opened them again. He was still there.

There had been a battle that day, in nearby Arapiles. It was one reason she had been able to sneak away for so long, since most people stayed close to their homes or fled to Salamanca to avoid stray bullets. And it was as well the reason she had taken a more circuitous route from the church than she normally did. Although there were some, like Hector, she suspected, who would monitor the battle from afar and when it was over sneak onto the battlefield to steal from the dead soldiers. She shivered and crossed herself at the thought of so many dead or dying men. War was such an ugly thing! When would it end?

"I'm not dead… yet."

She flinched and backed away. The soldier was looking directly at her. The shaky voice—weakened from his injuries, no doubt—came from the enemy soldier. But—she narrowed her eyes—he hadn't spoken French, but English! What was an English soldier doing in a French uniform?

He waved a white handkerchief and spoke in Spanish. "I'm not French. I'm an explorer officer for the British Army. Don't kill me, please, *señorita.* I have already been wounded once today."

"Were you in wounded in the battle?" she answered in English. Her knowledge of English was mostly limited to reading, so she wasn't certain he would understand her.

The soldier tried to shake his head and winced. That was when she saw the blood pooling on the ground near his head. "Nothing so noble. My horse reared at the sound of a cannon. My… head hit a rock when I fell off."

She looked around and saw no sign of a horse.

"Long gone. Not battle-trained. Stole him from a French bloke."

Catalina drew nearer and saw that he was shaking uncontrollably. Fearing that he might be dying, she hurriedly tore a large piece of her petticoat and knelt on the ground to wrap it around the wound to stem the flow of blood.

"I suppose that is where you got the uniform," she commented, hoping to keep him conscious. "I should go for help. Can you tell me the location of the surgeons' quarters?"

"Too dangerous," he said. "Could be some battle rage. Like Badajoz."

Catalina froze. News of the bloody massacre of soldiers and civilians alike in the aftermath of the siege only weeks before had spread quickly throughout the country, but it was only now that she realized her folly in passing so closely by a battlefield.

"Do you think so?" she asked, her gaze darting around her in search of raging soldiers.

"No. Perhaps. But it isn't safe here. You should go home."

She looked at the setting sun with concern. "But I can't leave you here. A passing vehicle is likely to run you down."

With much effort, he rolled onto his side. "Help me slide over there. Behind the bush."

Catalina gave him a skeptical look. "But that wound needs tending. And it gets cold at night… you are shivering already. You need food and water. And a doctor."

"No." With prodigious effort, he managed to sit up. "No one… must know I am here." He grinned, then winced. "Except you, of course. Too late."

Catalina's brain worked at lightning speed as she tried to think of a way to help the man. She couldn't take him home. Hector, even if he had any patriotic bone in his miserable body, wouldn't suffer him in the house and would not only not keep his mouth shut, but would probably try to sell him to the French, who would shoot him as a spy.

"Mire," she said. "If you can walk—even a little—I know of an old abandoned building on the other side of that hill. There's a stream not too far away. I could clean your wound and wash your bandages." *And keep you hidden for the night.*

He gave a deep sigh and finally nodded. "Let's do it." He looked doubtfully at her slender form. "I hope you are stronger than you appear, *señorita."*

"Catalina," she said as she bent to help him to his feet. He swayed for a moment, steadying himself by putting his arms around her shoulders.

"A pleasure, Catalina. I'm Rupert Ellsworth. And… thank you."

Catalina smiled. "You may thank me later, Señor Ellsworth. I suspect the old barn is undoubtedly already inhabited by a few rodents."

"Rupert, *por favor*. I'm willing to share."

By the time they arrived at the dilapidated old barn, Rupert was leaning heavily on Catalina, and she knew he was close to exhaustion.

"Stay here." She left him leaning against a tree and crept inside, trying to adjust her eyesight to the darkness and find a place for him to lie down and rest.

Of course, there would be rats, but she still gave a startled squeal when she heard a rustle of little feet darting away from her approach. It was too much to expect a pile of hay to soften the hardened dirt floor, but she did find a tattered old horse blanket that might be useful. It would be better rinsed off, she thought, wrinkling her nose at the smell of horse dung, but it would do for now.

"I don't know what else is here," she called, "but there are no *franceses.* And the *ratas* will not hurt you as long as you move around now and then to prove you are still alive."

"Thank you," he retorted. "Reassuring to know that I won't awake to find a finger or a toe chewed off as long as I am still breathing."

She giggled, surprised to realize that she was enjoying herself. "I've found a place for you to sleep near the window, but it is too dark to see much, so you should try to stay there until it's light enough to see if there are any sharp objects that could injure you further. No, wait for me!"

This last came when she saw him take a few wobbly steps on his own. "Just like a child," she chided. "You need a nurse to keep you from falling into mischief. Are all Englishmen so foolish?"

She felt him start to laugh and then stop, no doubt from the pain.

"All Spanish *señoritas*… are like you?" he managed. "Speak English? Tear their petticoats to shreds?"

She steadied him in the doorway to find the spot she had prepared. "A few more steps this way. Here. Sit down and put your head down this way."

Once he was on the ground, she announced that she was going to the stream for water. "Have you a-a vessel of some kind that I can use to bring back water for you?"

He grinned and dug out a flask from his pocket. "Cheap whisky. Drank it already."

She rolled her eyes. "So that explains it," she said as she took it out of his hands.

"*A propósito,*" she said as she headed toward the doorway. "I can read in English, French, Latin, and Greek."

"Ah. *Not* the typical Spanish *señorita*," she heard as she made her way toward the stream.

She caught herself humming as she stepped into cool water to fill the bottle. Typical? No, she was certainly not that. And for once, she was glad.

~

He loved the way she said his name. Trilling the first 'r' in the Spanish manner giving the 'e' the sound of a long 'a', which gave the name he'd never particularly liked much an exotic flare. Something the younger son of a gentleman farmer wasn't accustomed to feeling, even after more than a year of service with Wellington's forces as an explorer scout, a position he'd been offered because of his uncanny skill in languages, photographic memory, and ability to draw maps and terrain with meticulous detail.

He didn't get it because of elegant horsemanship, however, as he had reason to lament that day.

After his horse had been shot under him by one of Marmont's skirmishers, he'd scrambled to his feet and shot the fellow in the head with his pistol before he could reload. After he'd caught the dead man's frightened horse, the idea had come to him to put on the dead man's clothes and disguise himself as a French soldier to infiltrate the French line. Which might have worked had the wretched horse not reared up and sent him flying through the air to land on a rock with a very sharp edge.

Once he'd come to his senses, he'd realized the peril he was in. If he didn't die of the head wound, chances were that someone would come along and finish him off after recognizing his uniform. Few of the Spanish citizens in these parts supported the Bonaparte régime, considering them invaders, and even the *josefinos*, who initially supported Joseph Bonaparte's rule, had dwindled in number since the French troops desecrated churches and murdered priests.

Fortunately for him, however, it had been the lovely, tenderhearted Catalina who had come upon him and decided to help him in the nick of time. Unable to stop the flow of blood with his handkerchief, he'd have undoubtedly bled to death by morning if allowed to lie there overnight.

He drifted off for a time while she went to the stream, waking only when he felt her add another section of her petticoat to bind his head. When she tore off yet another piece and began to clean off some of the blood, he promised to buy her another petticoat when he recovered.

He couldn't remember what she said, except that she laughed, and his last conscious thought, before he drifted off into much-needed sleep, was that he wouldn't mind hearing that delightful sound the rest of his life.

The bandages had slowed—perhaps even stopped—the bleeding, and Catalina had cleaned the area as best she could. It worried her that he had lost consciousness. She poured a little water in his mouth from the flask, but when he didn't awaken, she capped it and left it by his side. She didn't like leaving him, but she couldn't stay there all night and besides, she needed to get supplies and medical advice. Abuela would help. She rose and reluctantly headed home.

What if he dies during the night? Alone, with no one to hold his hand?

She was so preoccupied by fear for this unknown man—this *Rupert*—that she forgot about Hector and the stable until her younger sister came out to meet her.

"Mamá says to tell you to get the stables done now, before Papá returns."

At Catalina's startled face: "Did you forget? What have you been doing, Catalina? Where have you been all afternoon? Surely the priest did not keep you past evening prayers?" Her eyes widened. "Did you go to see the battle? You must tell me all about it. Here, give me a rake and I will help you."

Startled back to reality, Catalina stared at her sister, who had never mucked stalls in her life. "You? Help muck stalls?"

"Well really," Ana María snapped. "I don't want Papá to be angry all evening any more than Mamá does. Or you either, I suppose. You'd best show me how to do it, and come up with some excuse for being away so long while you do."

Fortunately, both Consuelo and Hector were too excited about the riches he'd snagged from the battlefield dead to pay much attention to Catalina, and she was able to sneak away after *cena* without anyone the wiser.

Abuela was still awake, praying silently, rosary in hand, when Catalina entered their room. Catalina took out her own rosary and joined her, and when they had both finished, she confided her secret and asked for advice in treating the wounded soldier's head. Abuela's first husband had been a physician, and she'd learned much from assisting him with his calls.

"*¿Un soldado inglés?* Fell off his horse and hit his head?" Abuela chuckled. "At least the Spaniards can stay on their horses!"

But she listened intently as Catalina described the wound.

"You say it stopped bleeding? Let us hope so, because if not, he will be dead by morning." At Catalina's horrified gasp, she added, "If he lives, however, a fever will be the next hurdle." And she gave Catalina detailed instructions as to what to do and where she could find the supplies she needed.

"I can help with that, *mi hija.* Consuelo won't suspect anything if I rummage through her medicines since I have so many ailments."

Very early the next morning, armed with a basket of medicines, bandages, scissors, and some bread and wine, Catalina set off to help her injured Englishman. She'd slept only fitfully, terrified that he might be dying at any moment, but she couldn't leave while Hector was still guzzling his wine in the front room. By the time she heard his drunken footsteps on the stair and managed to escape, the old barn was visible in the light of dawn. Her heartbeat racing and her hands clammy with fear, she broke into a run and was breathing heavily when she stepped over the threshold.

He stirred slightly at the sound of the squeaky door. She closed her eyes briefly to give thanks to God that he still breathed. He would be a beautiful man, she thought, when his reddish-brown hair was not streaked with blood. But he was not conscious, and when she put a hand to his forehead, she realized that he had, as Abuela had warned, developed a fever. Fevers were dangerous. Hector's brother had died of a fever after a knife fight in the taberna. Beads of sweat formed on her upper lip as she became aware that the life of this man might well depend on *her.*

She swallowed hard and set to work. He wouldn't die so long as *she* had anything to do with it.

She managed to get him to swallow some willow bark tea as well as a spoonful of Abuela's favorite elixir, which she suspected contained some form of alcohol. She made several trips to the stream for water to cool off his fevered brow and try to force down his throat. She managed to lift his torso long enough to remove his shirt—blushingly pretending not to notice his muscled chest—and soaked it and every other piece of cloth she could find to use to cool his body. But when he began shivering and tossing and turning and mistook her for his mother, she feared her efforts were making him worse, and she crumpled to the floor, her knees to her chest, and rocked back and forth.

"I don't know what else to do, God. Don't let him die. Please don't die, R-Rupert Ellsworth."

Eventually she found the courage to clean around his head wound, clipping some of his hair, but being careful not to re-open the wound.

She didn't like to leave him, still hallucinating and alternately burning up and shivering, but she couldn't expect Abuela to cover for her much longer, and it was imperative to keep him hidden from Hector and Consuelo. When she did return home, she found Abuela standing in for her in the kitchen, dressed to go out, and ready to replace her at the soldier's side.

Catalina threw herself in Abuela's arms. "*¡Gracias, Abuelita!* He is so ill! But are you certain you can manage it?"

Abuela winked. "I'm not nearly so feeble as I claim to be, you know. Consuelo may be my own daughter, but she is a fool."

Catalina and her grandmother took turns tending their English soldier, who went in and out of consciousness, complaining of muscle aches as well as a horrendous headache. Once when Catalina took his hand and closed her eyes to pray, she felt a gentle squeeze in return and felt that his illness might at last be turning the corner.

With Abuela's assistance in concealing her absence, Catalina stayed with him throughout the night, bathing him with cool water and forcing medicine down his throat. By the time morning came, his fever seemed to have broken.

~

When he first awoke and looked into the startled blue eyes of the girl sitting nearby, he couldn't recall who she was or why he was there, but it all came back to him in a rush when she smiled and the concerned expression on her face turned to delighted relief.

"*¡Diós mío!* You are better, R-rupert—Señor Ellsworth!"

"Rupert," he said, finding it harder to speak than he expected. "And you are… Catalina."

She crossed herself. "We feared you would die. But you did not, *gracias a Diós!*"

"We?"

She smiled again, and he couldn't help noticing how beautiful she was when she smiled. Not that she wasn't pretty enough anyway. He wondered if she had a *novio*. In this country, she was of an age to be married and have a child or two.

She told him about how she and her *abuela* had between them managed to keep him alive for three days while his body raged with fever.

"Drink this."

He struggled to lift his head to make it easier to drink the water in the metal cup.

She chuckled. "It's so much easier to get water into you when you are awake. Many times I thought I might drown you, but Abuela said water was the best medicine."

It occurred to him that he was unclothed under the blanket and that the two ladies must have taken care of his most intimate needs.

"I suppose a mere thank you is inadequate," he said, struggling to get out the words. "Nursing me cannot have been a very pleasant task."

She shook her head and a few strands of jet black hair escaped the knot and caressed her lovely neck. "No need to thank me. God sent me. Padre told me that God would guide me if I listened to Him, and there you were, lying in the road, waiting for me!"

Rupert thought privately that he was just a very lucky man that she had come by when she did, but he did not wish to discourage her.

For an hour or so before dawn, she told him about herself, how she had been adopted into the Ordóñez family, her two sisters, and Abuela, who had read to her when she was small and taught her to read and write. She didn't say much about her parents, and considering that he already knew she'd had to keep his existence secret from them, it seemed likely that they were at best indifferent parents.

"Your sister is married? Do you not have a *novio* yourself?" For some reason, it seemed of paramount importance that he know the answer.

She flushed and shook her head, and he thought he'd never seen a prettier girl.

"*Matrimonio* is not what men want from me," she said sadly. "I am a *bastarda* and have no dowry. I thought perhaps I would become a nun and be free to do what I wish: read and study and help the poor."

He felt the urge to laugh at the thought of anyone believing the life of a nun as freedom, but as she spoke about the precious hours she had spent studying with the priest as she was growing up, it became clear that learning had become both an escape from a life of drudgery and a door to the world outside her tame little village.

Abuela, when she arrived for her shift, provided little more information about his angel, which was how he was beginning to think of Catalina. He could tell that she loved Catalina and despised her son-in-law. She feigned a stern look when he protested about the gruel she lifted to his lips, demanding *pan* and *carne,* and understood perfectly when she rolled her eyes and called him a *cerdo.* Grinning, he made a pig sound, and the two of them chuckled.

In the days that followed, as he recovered his strength, he made more discoveries about his beautiful guardian angel. He learned from Abuela about Catalina's birth, her mother's memory loss and subsequent death in childbirth, and how her daughter and son-in-law had come to adopt her and then come to neglect her after the birth of their own daughters.

"I became her mother," Abuela had told him. "But I could not always protect her from Hector."

She never mentioned any examples of Hector's cruelty, but Rupert heard enough to wish to bash the scoundrel's head in.

She, too, thought Catalina's idea of becoming a nun was a foolish one. "She is a good *católica,* my Catalina, but she is far too rebellious. No, I do not believe her future lies anywhere in Las Torres."

Rupert had a brief thought of taking Catalina with him to England, but he put it out of his mind immediately. He was committed to Wellington's Army for months yet, and besides, what would he do with her in England? As a younger son, he had no home of his own, and no income, unless he found a government job of some sort. And while he found it quite appealing to imagine having Catalina as his wife, he knew it wouldn't do. She was, as her Abuela mentioned, a devoted Catholic, who would be a fish out of water in Anglican England. Her questionable background didn't help either. A voice inside suggested that the appearance of an exotic beauty on English soil might actually be a welcome boon to the pompous English Society, but he dismissed the thought as whimsy. He couldn't get leg-shackled for years yet. And when he did, his bride would be a suitable English rose, as he had promised his father.

And why was he even thinking that way about her? The worn gray gown she wore day after day did nothing for her coloring and covered her like a nun. From time to time he could see hints of the curves underneath when she bent over him or twisted around to reach for the bucket or a clean cloth. Other than the slight flush and avoiding his gaze when she washed him or dealt with his bodily needs, she seemed to think of him as a patient rather than a man.

And *that* bothered him more than it should have.

"Catalina," her grandmother said to her one night as they were settling down to bed, "you must guard your heart against this man. The fact that you are doing God's work does not mean that you will not both be tempted to take it further than is wise."

Catalina's pulse quickened. "*¡Ridículo!* The Englishman does not think of me in that way!"

But she averted her gaze, recalling the heated looks in his eyes on occasion when he observed her body. She had seen such looks before and knew they indicated sexual interest.

Abuela raised her eyebrows. "Does he not? He is a man, isn't he?" Then she softened her tone. "He is a good man, *mi hija,* and he means you no harm, but if you let down your guard and show him too much affection, he may not be able to restrain himself." She sighed heavily. "If I had warned my daughter sufficiently, she might not have ended up with a *borracho* like Hector. The urge to mate is very powerful."

Catalina caught her breath at the thought of being the wife of the Englishman. She was sure he would not be a brutish husband like Hector. He would take her away and cherish her…

She forced herself back to reality. She was completely unsuitable to be the wife of a man whose brother, she had discovered, would one day become an English *vizconde*. And if she were not careful, she could lose her virginity and even be left with a child, in which case Hector would toss her out and she would have nowhere to go…

She swallowed hard. As much as she wished she were out of Hector's control, *that* was not the way to do it. Although the thought of having a child with Rupert had its appeal… No!

"I will take care, Abuela."

~

As he recuperated his strength from the heavy loss of blood, Rupert became more and more curious about Catalina's family. The time was fast approaching when he would be well enough to return to his commander. While he was eager to get back into action, he dreaded the thought of never seeing her again. All because he owed her his life, of course, and wished he could repay the favor. Not because he had any special regard for her.

He practiced getting to his feet and walking a few steps, and one evening, when Catalina had departed, he followed her, keeping himself at a discreet distance.

It probably wasn't more than a half-mile, but he had not fully recovered physically, so when she crossed the threshold into the rundown farmhouse, he collapsed into a heap behind a shrub and tried to catch his breath while he observed the place his Angel called home.

The Ordóñez holding wasn't much different from the majority of farms he had seen in that area of Spain, perhaps a bit more neglected than most. The war had had a deleterious effect on the Spanish people in recent years. Money was scarce and food scarcer. He'd seen desperate soldiers break into homes like this one and take every last morsel of food, to the extent of slaughtering the cow that was the only source of milk for the children. He wondered what Catalina's life had been like, living with a drunken sot of a father in war-torn Spain.

Loud arguing brought him back to the present. The sound of a man's angry voice, the words *ladrona* (thief) and *puta* (whore) and objects being thrown amidst cries of pain drove him to his feet. Was it Catalina Hector was beating? Heat flushed through his body and he almost rushed in to rescue her before he realized that he was in no condition to rescue anyone. He rose to his feet, fists clenched, desperately wishing he had his normal strength back so that he could send the worthless brute Hector off to the netherworld where he belonged.

"¡Vaya!"

Abuela crept up behind him and pulled at him to leave. "You cannot help her. You will only get yourself killed! Go!"

At his hesitation, she insisted, "You cannot intercede. Go, before he sees you!"

At that moment, Catalina, her face swollen and her sleeve torn, fled the house, heading for the barn. A red-faced Hector stood in the doorway cursing loudly, but not attempting to pursue her.

"Catalina is strong. She will be all right. It will be worse for her if you are discovered."

Hector turned and walked back into the house, knocking something over in his anger.

Rupert was trembling with anger, frustrated that he couldn't give the scoundrel what was coming to him or even whisk Catalina away from that miserable place. He wasn't accustomed to standing around and watching women be mistreated. Even at Badajoz he had managed to hide two women from rampaging soldiers intent on rape and destruction. How utterly humiliating that he couldn't do anything to help his Angel when she most needed him.

Abuela finally persuaded him to return to the barn, promising to bring him news of Catalina in the morning. Before he left, she warned him against taking advantage of her granddaughter.

"Catalina has had a hard life, señor, as have many of our countrywomen in recent years. She is one of the strong ones. She will survive. But you will not do her any favors if you make to her promises that you cannot keep, or worse, if you leave her with a babe in her belly. If you care for her at all beyond the physical, you will not encourage her to hope she has a future with you."

Rupert understood what she was saying loud and clear. It was nothing more that what he had been telling himself all along. His father had raised his sons to eschew the idea of marrying for love or affection. Love didn't last, he expostulated, using his own failed marriage as a perfect example.

The elder Ellsworth had fallen in love with a Creole beauty in Barbados, brought her to England where she was utterly miserable, and ultimately, some years later, run off with a ship's captain and died when the ship was attacked by pirates. His father's bitterness stemmed from heartbreak, Rupert knew. Although very young, he recalled the look on his parents' faces when they looked at each other, the frequent embraces, secret smiles. But he also remembered how the delicate beauty suffered in the cold winters and pined for the warm sandy beaches she'd loved. His father's refusal to take her back for a visit caused a strain in their marriage that had ultimately led to tragedy.

Rupert and his older brother Simon had heard the story many times, and while they'd loved their mother, neither wanted to find themselves in their father's situation. Life was about hard work, duty and honor, respecting the family traditions, and passing them on to the next generation. This was true especially for Simon, who, as his father's heir, was being groomed for a viscountcy someday, as their father stood heir to his own brother, the current viscount, who had no children.

Rupert wondered about Simon. He wasn't much of a correspondent, being an outdoorsman and horse-mad like all Englishmen. Simon would have jumped at the chance to join Wellington's army had their father been open to it, but their father insisted that the heir remain safely at home and only "the spare" exposed to danger.

A good thing indeed you aren't here, dear brother. Life is a fragile thing, especially anywhere near a battlefield. And I would have died from falling off my horse had it not been for the courageous Catalina. My Angel.

But she was not his. He rammed his fist into the barn door hard enough to poke a hole through the weathered old plank.

"What did you do to your hand, Rupert?"

Catalina, sporting the beginnings of bruises on her eye and arms, had managed to steal away after Hector's departure for work, bringing him bread, ham, grapes, and wine in spite of Hector's directive that she be limited to bread and water for two days for her sin of stealing food. With Hector gone, Abuela had kept Consuelo otherwise occupied while Catalina raided the larder and escaped from her room.

Rupert—oh how she loved to say his name—grimaced and mumbled something about running into the door in the dark, but it didn't ring true. No doubt he was impatient to get back to his scouting duties.

She herself didn't even want to think about it. His presence had given her life meaning beyond her humdrum existence with the Ordóñez family. What had the priest said to her? That he believed God had something special in mind for her, and that she should simply wait for Him to reveal it. Could Rupert possibly be part of His plan for her? She was more than a little in love with him—what girl wouldn't be?—but it could also be a test of her moral compass. How did one know the difference?

They were sitting under a tree as the morning sun chased away the chill of the night and began its ascent in the sky. Rupert was ravenously hungry after so many days of water and gruel, and she liked to watch him eat. He would look much better in the British uniform, regal red or even green, she decided, French blue not showing his burnished hair to advantage. She'd looked into his brown eyes on many occasions, and she liked the gentleness and strength she saw in them when he looked at her. Although… sometimes she could swear there was something else there as well… a heat that both excited and frightened her. He was a good man, but he was a man. And men liked her, she knew. She'd never felt anything but loathing for their catcalls and lurid suggestions and was careful to avoid the *tabernas* where they congregated. But this man—her Rupert, as she thought of him—he incited a very different feeling inside her.

"You should eat as well, Catalina. You are too thin."

Ah, there was that look in his eyes as he appraised her body. Her heart began to beat faster. It was almost as though he could see her curves beneath the drab gray frock that covered her from the neck down. She knew that look well. He was interested. If he knew that she shared his feelings… She closed her eyes and prayed for strength.

Their fingertips touched when she accepted a chunk of bread from him, and she felt a tingling that caused her heart to miss a beat. She bit into the bread hurriedly, looking away quickly to the rickety barn.

"I heard it rain last night. Did you get wet, Señor Rupert?"

"Rupert. I like the way you say my name."

She gave him a quick glance. He was still looking at her that way. She took a deep breath, and swallowed nervously when she saw his gaze move down to her chest.

"There was a dry spot in the corner, but the leaks turned the floor into a muddy mess. I took a bath in the stream, but this uniform is filthy."

"Perhaps I could wash it for you—" She spoke without thinking and flushed.

He grinned. "While I walk around in this wretched blanket?" He pointed to the torn and moth-eaten fabric underneath him. "Too bad that worthless horse got away with my saddlebag. What I wouldn't give to be wearing my own uniform when I return to camp. As it is, I'll be fortunate if my own compatriots don't shoot me on sight."

Catalina's hand flew to her chest. "*¡Diós mío!* They will not do that, will they?"

He put down the bread and took her hand in his. "No, of course not. I was jesting, Catalina. They won't recognize me at first, but it's highly unlikely they will shoot an unarmed man."

He reached up and lightly touched her bruised eye. "Catalina, it is your safety that concerns me more. That man you call father is a monster! If I had my rifle I would shoot him for you, or run him through with the sword I pinched from the bloody Frog. I cannot bear the thought of leaving you to his brutality."

Catalina shook her head. "His blows no longer have the power to hurt me. I have eighteen years' experience learning how to deal with him. And I have Abuela."

He shook his head. "Your grandmother won't be around forever. I don't trust you in the same house with that animal. I wouldn't put it past him to… meddle with your person, Catalina."

Catalina shrugged. "Consuelo will not bear that," she said evasively.

He narrowed his eyes. "He *has* made overtures to you! That-that swine!" He slammed his fist into the ground.

"No, no, Rupert!" she cried, covering his fist with her hands. "It is just the way he looks at me sometimes. Nothing more than that. I can manage him," she insisted. "God will help me."

Rupert snorted. "I wish I had your faith."

Catalina stared down at her empty hands. "There is nothing you can do, Rupert. You must return to your comrades and fight the *franceses*."

At his look of pain, she seized his hands and squeezed them tightly. "There are many girls like me. You cannot save us all! You feel a responsibility for me because I helped you… and because you understand my situation. But I am no worse off than many girls here—better than some. I will survive, I promise you. *Diós me ayudará*."

He stared at her intently, flames practically shooting out of his eyes.

"Is that all it is, *mi ángel?* Gratitude? Responsibility? I don't believe it… and I don't think you do either!"

He leaned toward her and gripped her shoulders, drawing her

closer until their noses nearly touched. Her nerve endings tingled at his nearness, and she licked her lips nervously.

That seemed to inflame him even more. He tilted his head and clamped his lips down on hers. At once all the longings pent up inside her surged outward, and all she could think of was the pleasure of his lips and his hands and the intensity of the hunger in his eyes as they kissed. Her hands went instinctively to his hair; she marveled at its softness as she ran her hands through it. He tore his lips away with a groan and moved his hands down her arms, where he gently kissed the bruises and looked at her with tormented eyes.

"How dare he strike my Angel! Because you *are* mine, Catalina! We belong together… you must feel it too!"

Por Diós, she did! Being in his arms was like heaven, and she delighted in the feel of his mouth on her skin, feeling lightheaded as he loosened the laces on her bodice so that he could kiss his way down her chest to the valley between her breasts. Her fingers ached to touch him as well, and she had his shirt halfway unbuttoned before the sound of a galloping horse caused them to break apart in alarm.

The rider passed by in the distance, not seeing them, but they both saw that he was a British soldier.

~

That was when he knew he had to go. By this time, his commander had found his dead horse and given him up for dead as well. He rose to his feet and offered his hand to her, pulling her toward him for a last embrace.

"I must go," he whispered against her lips.

She tightened her arms around his neck. "You cannot! You are still weak!" she protested, her voice shaking. "Stay one more day, and I will go with you!"

The very thought of his rough comrades getting a glimpse of Catalina's beauty made him shudder.

"No, Catalina. I will go on my own two feet. The commander won't send me on any long treks right away. He will be relieved to see me alive." Colonel McIntosh had once told him the task he hated most—other than losing men in battle—was writing letters to the fathers and mothers of the fallen. Surely he had not got around to doing that as of yet, but he would soon, if Rupert did not appear.

Catalina sobbed into his waistcoat. Rupert took her wet face between his hands and gazed at her tenderly.

"I will return for you, *mi ángel*. I promise I will come back and take you away from here, to a place where you can be safe. I will not rest easy as long as you are in the control of that brute."

He felt like a heel. Every gentlemanly instinct cried for him to be her knight in shining armor and ride off with her into the sunset on his white charger. But he wasn't a knight, had no armor—shining or otherwise—and had nothing but his own two legs, and they were still decidedly shaky.

Even more, he was honor-bound to return to duty. The soldier that had just passed had been headed for Las Torres, either seeking supplies or news of him, or quite possibly both.

"Please be careful," she pleaded as he tucked the wineskin into his belt and the few remaining items of food into his pockets. "Stay out of the way of the French bullets."

He kissed her tenderly on the lips. "I'll do my best. And I'll endeavor not to fall off any more horses as well."

That same evening

"Catalina, *mi hija,* do you still cry for Señor Ellsworth? I feared this would happen. First love can be so traumatic for a young girl."

Catalina sniffed into her pillow. She loved her grandmother with a passion, but there were times when she wished she could withdraw from the world and mourn in privacy.

"Abuela, please… "

Her grandmother snorted. "You think your problems are unique, *señorita?* Nearly everyone has such a story to tell. As I do."

Catalina propped her head up with her elbow and looked across the bed at the older woman. "You were in love with Abuelo?"

Abuela's eyes softened in the moonlight. "After we married, *sí.* But my first love was Raúl, the blacksmith's son. He was a big, strong one. I used to watch him work the metal in the fire, without his *camisa.* He caught me once and winked. I was lost."

Catalina smiled in spite of herself. "You did *not* do that, Abuela!"

Abuela raised her eyebrows. "You do not believe me, *niña?* I do not lie to you. I would have married Raúl in a heartbeat."

"Why didn't you?"

"My father would not allow it. Said that Raúl was a Don Juan like his father. Instead, I married my dear Hugo—*Diós le bendiga*—and learned what real love really was."

"What is it, Abuela?"

Abuela sighed and patted Catalina's head. "It is more than the physical, *niña.* More than what you have known with Señor Ellsworth in those few days you had together."

Catalina laid her head back onto the pillow, lost in thought for several minutes. Finally, she got the courage to ask the question that had been tormenting her since she had watched Rupert walk away.

"Abuela, do you think he will come back for me?"

Abuela's brow furrowed. "Ah, *cariña,* that remains to be seen. If God so wills it, he will return. If not, there is something better for you."

Catalina drew in a breath and then released it. Was there anything better for her than Rupert? She couldn't imagine what it could be.

"Abuela?"

"Sí, *mi niña?*" came the sleepy voice from the other side of the bed.

"Did Raúl turn out to be a Don Juan as your father predicted?"

Abuela's body quaked with laughter, shaking the bed. "Not at all. He married my best friend and they had fifteen children and were very happy until she died a few years ago."

Catalina sat up and grinned at her grandmother. "So you are both widowed? Perhaps you should seek him out, Abuela!"

Abuela threw a pillow at her. "*¡Por Dios, no!* The man must have a hundred grandchildren by now, and I have enough *problemas* with the three I have!"

Following the victory at Salamanca, the British forces continued to tangle with the French for some weeks, until they were finally pushed back to Ciudad Rodrigo. Rupert and his fellow scouts roved through the region for information on the French troops to bring back to Wellington and his advisors. For much of that time, the French held Salamanca, and Rupert wondered how Catalina and her *abuela* were faring in their little village. He dreamed of her often, sometimes fantasizing about the feel of her soft body against his, the sweetness of her lips, the image of her silky dark hair against his pillow… And then there were the dreams where she was being beaten by her drunken father, or even worse—in one dream he saw her face on one of the women he'd seen viciously raped at Badajoz—and she was calling for him to save her—in vain, because he was not there.

So often he was tempted to return to the village to reassure himself that she was safe, but his commander kept him busy, and besides, he had nothing new to say to her. He was still duty-bound to the British Army. Catalina was strong, he knew, but that blasted father of hers—he always clenched his fists when he recalled the bruises on Catalina's face and arms—was capable of anything. And then there were all the soldiers—English, French, Portuguese, Prussian—who in the heat of battle were likely to commit any number of atrocities, as he had reason to remember.

He needed to get her away from there, to England. And soon.

Chapter 2

September 21, 1812
Santiago de Compostela, Spain

"Colonel McIntosh? Welcome to the Convent of San Francisco."

The woman who addressed him was short and spare with a youthful face and kind eyes. He doubted she weighed more than seven stone dripping wet. Not at all the sort of person he imagined a mother superior to be. But his idea of a disciplinarian came from the military. In any case, neither Lord Wellington, nor Napoleon, for that matter, were particularly tall, nor did they need to be to inspire obedience.

Tobias rose from his seat in the foyer and bowed politely.

"Thank you for seeing me, *Madre Superiora*. I have come to beg your assistance in a matter of great personal importance."

"I shall be pleased to assist you if I am able, *Coronel*. Please follow me."

He waited until she was seated at her desk and he settled on a wooden chair facing her.

"Nineteen years ago I saw my wife board a ship to England. We'd been working to transport noble families condemned to the guillotine to safety when she became *enceinte*, and I decided she and the child should go to my family until I could join them."

He felt a knot in his belly as he always did when he recalled that poignant day when he had sent her off to her death—or at least assumed he had. Until he had heard of a nun who had escaped to Ireland from a convent in Octeville-sur-mer following the abolition of Christianity in France. In her memoirs, she told of a young girl dressed as a man who was found on a beach soon after the sinking of the *Chasseresse.* A pregnant woman who had lost her memory. A woman who *had* to be his Justine!

"Sister Margaret indicated that the woman they called Étoile was evacuated to Spain, to this convent," he concluded, turning a hopeful gaze to the woman before him.

"You are, of course, too young to know of her personally, but if you could direct me to someone older… Or perhaps she is here…" He held his breath, hardly daring to believe he could be so close.

Mother Superior gave an understanding nod. "I am not so young as I appear, *Coronel.* I was a novitiate in those days, and I remember Étoile and the French sisters when they were forced to leave their home. They did not remain here long, however, as our establishment had insufficient capacity for all. I believe that the unfortunate young woman accompanied Soeur Agnès to our sisters in Salamanca."

She rang a bell, and a novitiate entered, bowing her head to him and the abbess. *"¿Sí, Madre Superiora?"*

Following a chain of rapid Spanish, the young nun returned with a taller nun whose wrinkled face showed her advanced age.

The Mother Superior introduced them and briefly explained his mission. Hermana Ana did not speak English, but the abbess, translating for her, confirmed that the poor, afflicted *señorita* had gone to Salamanca with her fierce protector.

But then she hesitated, her face showing pity, and fear for what she had to say jolted his body.

The Abbess, likewise, turned a somber face to him. "Hermana Ana tells me that your wife—if she is indeed the woman called Étoile—succumbed to complications of childbirth while she was in Salamanca. My sympathies, *Coronel*."

Tobias covered his face with his hands and took a deep breath. Too late. Nineteen—no eighteen-odd—years too late. But then he looked up.

"The child?" he asked in a trembling voice, hardly daring to hope.

Hermana Ana did not need anyone to translate the words. "*Hembra*," she said with a smile. "Étoile had a little girl."

Two days later
Ordóñez farm

Catalina wiped a hand over her forehead as she finished mucking out the barn. Hector would have nothing of which to complain when he returned for the day. At least nothing in the barn. The milk cow and the two pigs lolled around the farmyard and Hector's horse would have plenty of oats and water waiting for him.

She left the barn, heading for the stream for a wash before starting the *cena* when she heard horses approaching. Hector? she thought in a sudden panic. He should not be home for another two hours! And who would his companion be? Hector's only friends were drunks from the *taberna*, and he'd more likely punch them than bring them home for dinner. But it was not Hector, she realized as the travelers came into view. One was a redcoat. Rupert? Her heart raced. Had her *soldado* come to rescue her at last?

But no, he was an older man, she saw with a sinking heart.

And his companion was dressed in the manner of a Spanish public official, his navy blue garb embellished with gold buttons and colorful medals.

The redcoat was looking at her with a curious expression, seemingly unable to speak. Or he thought she couldn't understand English. In any case, he had too many insignias on his uniform to be the sort who would be sent to steal supplies for the troops. She'd been through such experiences before, but only from French soldiers, never English. Although she supposed they might resort to such tactics if they were hungry enough.

The other man introduced himself as a magistrate and the redcoat as Colonel McIntosh, and asked to see Hector Ordóñez. Or Catalina Ordóñez, if she were present.

"I am Catalina Ordóñez," she said, feeling increasingly concerned. "My father is not here at present." Hector had had his run-ins with the law, but what could they possibly want with *her?*

"I knew it!" The redcoat jumped down from his horse and came toward her. Tears were streaming down his face. "She's the image of Justine. I can hardly believe it! Finding her again after so many years. A miracle of miracles!"

Catalina backed away. Who *was* this man, this Colonel McIntosh? And who was Justine? She blinked to make sure she wasn't dreaming. No, it was real.

The British officer stopped. "Don't be afraid, my dear. I would never hurt you. I'm your father, come to find you after so many years of believing you dead. I thought you drowned along with your mother. But then to discover that you, at least, are living still… I hardly know what to say."

Catalina's body tensed as she peered into the newcomer's bright blue eyes and saw near duplicates of her own. How could he possibly be her father? Why would he have bothered to seek out an illegitimate child. Unless… She had so many questions, but she was too emotionally wrought to verbalize them. Some part of her acknowledged his assertion of their kinship, and when he opened his arms, she ran into them.

"Papa." Her tears wet his coat, and she remembered her bedraggled state. "I'm soiling your coat," she said in English.

"Soil it all you wish—" he started to say, and then widened his eyes. "You speak English," he said in amazement.

"And French. I can read in Latin and Greek," she boasted. "The Padre foretold that I would need this knowledge someday."

"My daughter. A scholar," he said in a shaky voice. "I have a daughter. A grown-up daughter." He hugged her as though he would never let her go. Finally he released her and regarded her with excitement in his eyes.

"There is so much to do. So much to say. You must go to England and meet your aunts and cousins. And your grandmother. She will be over the moon—"

"What is this? Take your hands off my daughter, *señor!*"

Consuelo appeared in the doorway, hostility written on her face.

The magistrate stepped forward, pulling out a sheaf of papers from under his coat. "She is not your daughter, Señora Ordóñez. Legally, she is Catriona Mary McIntosh, daughter of Tobias Andrew McIntosh, Earl of Dumfries, and his wife Justine Marie Beaudreau, daughter of the late Comte and Comtesse d'Audet."

Consuelo clutched her chest and would have fallen had not her youngest daughter been there to catch her.

"You're the daughter of a *conde?*" Ana María said in disbelief as she helped her mother to her feet. "I don't believe it."

Nobody believed it, not even Catalina herself, until they had all had a chance to review the official documents that her father—her *father!*—had brought with him—signed affidavits from nuns who had known her mother and witnessed her birth, her parents' marriage lines, even a ring Justine had given Soeur Agnès before her death that turned out to be inscribed with Justine's mother's name. The magistrate was there to verify His Lordship's right to reclaim his daughter.

As delighted as she was to have a father—a real one—and know that she was his legitimate child and would be taken away from the Ordóñez family forever, she still had misgivings. This life was all she had ever known. England seemed far away, and she wasn't sure how eagerly her father's relatives would welcome her—for all appearances a Spanish peasant, who spoke English hesitantly and with an accent, and was devoutly Catholic. Tobias McIntosh seemed to be a kind and doting father, but she didn't really *know* him. At least here in Las Torres she knew what to expect.

She wasn't really close to her sisters—they had been encouraged to disdain her as a *bastarda* as their parents did—but they were the only family she'd ever known. Other than Abuela.

And there was the rub. Abuela had been ill of late, confined to her bed for most of the day, only able to leave it when Catalina was there to provide support. Once she was gone, Catalina feared her grandmother would not be properly cared for. In tears, she begged her to come with them to England.

"*¡Diós mío!* What would I do in *Inglaterra*? No, I belong here, *mi hija,* with my daughter and granddaughters. Consuelo is not without all feeling toward me, *tú sabes*. She is not you, Catalina, but you must go with your father and fulfill your destiny."

As for Rupert, Catalina hadn't heard from him for two

months. She didn't have any idea where he was or whether he had any intention of returning for her. He'd meant to at the time—of that she had no doubt—but war had a way of monopolizing one's attention, and he could be tied up in this one for years yet. The one thing she *did* have was a real, live father who wanted to claim her and make amends for the past. With a heavy heart, she wrote a long letter to him explaining what had happened and how to reach her, leaving it in Abuela's keeping, should he ever return.

It was all in God's hands now.

She had said her goodbyes, packed up her meager belongings and was ready to mount her father's horse by the time Hector returned, drunk and spoiling for a fight. His first reaction—once he realized that Tobias McIntosh was a wealthy English lord—was to demand money to reimburse him for all he had spent on that *bastarda perezosa*. Her father, who by this time had heard about Hector's brutality, gave him a punch that sent him tumbling to the earth, warning him never to call his daughter a bastard ever again.

Catalina—now to be Lady Catriona—was shaking with emotion when she mounted the horse behind her father and left the Ordóñez farm behind. Forever.

December 3, 1812
Ciudad Rodrigo, Spain

"You're to return to Surrey immediately," Rupert was told when he arrived at the command post. Since his commander had departed several weeks earlier on an urgent family matter, he reported directly to the Earl of March, Charles Gordon-Lennox, one of Wellington's aides-de-camp. "Supplies are due to arrive in Porto next week; I'm sure you can get a berth for the return trip."

He clapped a hand on Rupert's shoulder. "We are sorry to see you go. You have done your country great service in this godforsaken war."

Rupert tore off the seal of the letter handed to him and scanned his aunt's hastily scribbled words. A sudden coldness jolted his core when he became aware of the reason for the summons—his brother was dead. Killed instantly by a fall from his horse during a frenzied rush at a fox hunt. His head burst open when it landed on a rock.

Rupert put his head in his hands and stifled the urge to laugh hysterically. He'd suffered a similar injury only a few months before and survived. Not to mention that he'd had many close calls during his stint in the Peninsula—during a bloody war, for God's sake! And he was the *spare!* Simon, the heir, had been obligated to stay behind where it was safe. Safe!

It should have been me. I never wanted to be tied to the estate, or inherit a title. Damn you, Simon. You should have been more careful.

His aunt wrote that the tragic news had caused his father to suffer an attack of apoplexy, which left him unable to manage his affairs, which were currently under the supervision of his older brother's—the viscount's—steward. The viscountess wrote:

Both my husband and your father entreated me to write to the Duke himself to request that he excuse you from further service due to your father's health and the pressing needs of the estate. I am confident that he will do so, as he cannot fail to understand how devastating it would be to all of us to lose the one remaining heir to the viscountcy.

Later, when he folded the letter and put it in his jacket pocket and shook hands with the earl, it occurred to him that he could now fulfill his promise to take Catalina away from her intolerable situation. His heart pounded with anticipation at seeing her once again. Was she well? Had her beastly father been knocking her around again? He'd spent many sleepless nights feeling like a heel for leaving her in peril, but other than marrying her out of hand and bringing her to camp with him…

He shuddered. Why *hadn't* he insisted on marrying her? He could have at least spared her several months of anxiety. True, he'd had nothing to offer her then, and life in an army camp was no place for a woman, really, but—it was certainly better than what she had.

All because he feared his father's disapproval. But Rupert wasn't his father. And Catalina wasn't his delicate, island-bred mother. And that was when Rupert knew with certainty that his strong, vibrant Spanish angel was the right sort of wife for him, not some docile little English rose with no thought in her head beyond modistes and milliners.

He saddled his horse and set out for Las Torres without a moment's delay.

"Catalina is not here, señor. She is dead."

It was Catalina's sister, no older than thirteen or fourteen, who answered the door.

Rupert did not believe it. He pushed past the girl and forced his way into the house. "Where is she? Where is Catalina? I know she is not dead. Catalina!"

Unless Hector had become too rough with her… But no, he refused to believe that. Catalina was too vigorous and bursting with life to have lost it so soon. She would have fought to the death. Death? His legs weakened with fear.

He thrust open the door to the room that he was told had been Catalina's. It was empty. No clothing in the clothespress. No bed coverings on the mattress. No hint of any inhabitant.

"Abuela," he said. Hadn't Catalina shared a room with her grandmother? "I must speak to your grandmother. She will tell me where I can find Catalina."

The girl's chin trembled. "Abuela has gone to God. We are in mourning for her," she added, indicating her black gown. "And Catalina too," she added hastily.

"How did she die?" Rupert asked suspiciously.

The girl wiped her hand on her sleeve. "She was old. How do you think she died?" she almost screamed at him. "Who are you and how do you know Catalina… or Abuela?" Her eyes narrowed. "You were her *amante!* Papá said she was nothing more than a *puta!*"

By that time Consuelo had come in from the barn and had picked up a pot to defend herself from the unknown soldier.

"*¡Mamá!*" the girl screamed. "He is Catalina's *amante,* come to take her away! I told him she was dead, but he does not believe me!"

Consuelo lowered the pot, but didn't put it down. "My daughter is truthful. Catalina fell ill with a fever and died weeks ago. Would you like to see her grave?"

Rupert's hands turned clammy. No! It couldn't be! God would not be so cruel as to take both his brother and his beloved! But how else could her absence be explained?

When he knelt before the gravestones—one that read *María Augusta Romero de Gómez* with the date 8 Octubre 1812—and the other *María Catalina Ordóñez y Gómez* dated 23 Septiembre 1812—he slammed his fist on the ground.

Why, God? Why did you do this? Was it not enough to take Simon from me? Why did you also have to take Catalina? She loved you and trusted you… for what? She deserved so much more than the short, miserable life you granted her. I would have taken her away to a better life, cherished her, loved her!

Finally he wiped his eyes and rose to his feet. Keeping his eyes hooded, he pulled out a coin and handed it to Consuelo.

"For flowers. For Catalina and her… Abuela," he said.

And he walked back to his horse and rode off. Catalina was gone. Simon was gone. And life as he knew it was about to take a drastic turn.

March 1, 1815
Brussels, Belgium
The Countess of Covington's Ball

"My dear Lady Catriona, it is so refreshing to meet an English lady who speaks French as well as you do. Most of the ladies here have the most atrocious accents! *Quelle horreur!* How they *murder* our beautiful language! But you… you have a most charming English accent. Most unusual."

The Baronne de Ligny, her towering, powdered hair an indication of her advanced age, smiled approvingly at Catriona from across the small table.

Little does she know that my accent is not English at all, but Spanish.

In the two years—nearly three now—since she had been whisked from poverty in Spain to a lavish life among the English *ton,* her English had improved considerably, but still retained a hint of her foreign origins. While many declared her accent "charming" and "original," to some—a few of the highsticklers—it was a reminder of her foreign upbringing.

To the French, however—or the Belgians, as was the case here—her French was fluent enough to pass muster even among the most pompous. Perhaps because her father, the Earl of Dumfries, had received a medal from Louis XVIII for his heroism in the aftermath of the Revolution. It also didn't hurt that her mother had been the daughter of a *comte* and that she herself held the title of *Comtesse d'Audet* in her stead.

And because the English had a tendency to speak other languages so abominably—excluding her father, who had a French mother himself.

"I hear His Grace *le Duc* is on his way here from Vienna" the *baronne* commented. "The news of the escape of *le Petit Caporal* from the island has caused a bit of *désordre* among the English, *n'est-ce pas?*" She thrust her shoulders back. "I knew the magnificent Bonaparte would be back. It is Destiny."

Catriona chuckled. To say that the *baronne* was an odd duck was an understatement. A Belgian lady of aristocratic descent who still dressed in the style of Marie Antoinette from two decades ago, she was a fervent supporter of the French invader. Eccentric she might be, but she was invited everywhere because of her noble blood. And because her son-by-marriage was a close friend of the Bourbon king, who was nothing more than an impostor according to the *baronne*.

"*Tiens! Ma chère,* it is Étienne Marchand, the son of the Comte d'Artois, coming this way. I believe he wishes to dance with you!" She leaned forward. "They say he is looking for a rich wife."

Catriona closed her eyes. *Not another one!* While in London she had been declared a diamond of the first water—where had that term come from?—her murky background and devotion to Catholicism were enough to dissuade all but the fortune-hunters from offering for her. Among the French and Belgian nobility—most of whom were Catholic and poverty-stricken—she was in great demand, however.

"May I have this dance, mademoiselle la comtesse?"

"Lady Catriona, *s'il vous plaît.* I would be honored to dance with you, *monsieur.*"

"You dance divinely, my lady," he said as they performed the intricate steps of the quadrille.

She bowed her head in acknowledgment.

"You are much admired," he said with an appreciative gleam in his eyes. "They are all saying the Lady Catriona is the most beautiful lady here."

Catriona gritted her teeth. By this time she was accustomed to flattery of this sort, but it never failed to cause a bitter taste in her mouth. Having grown up with two frocks to her name—one to wear and one to wash—she abhorred the excesses of Society. "That money could have fed half of Las Torres for a year!" she had protested to her father upon catching sight of the first dressmaker's bill. But she was an earl's daughter and must dress as such, he'd insisted. And he was so proud of her, so determined to give her everything he could not during her first eighteen years.

She loved him dearly, but the things he wanted for her were not things she wished for herself. Marriage perhaps—she loved children and longed for some of her own. But none of the gentlemen she'd met thus far appealed to her. Not the way her Rupert had done.

She wondered what had happened to him, if he had fallen in the war or simply forgotten her. Either possibility made her feel a hollowness in her chest. If he had come, Abuela would have given him the letter. Although… she hadn't received any word of

Abuela at all since leaving Spain, even though she'd sent many letters. Which was another reason to worry. Surely her grandmother had recovered from her illness by now! Unless…

The music stopped, and the dancers bowed to each other. Monsieur Marchand led her to her stepmother, who greeted her enthusiastically.

"There you are, Catriona, my dear. I wanted to introduce you to Lady Penworthy, who was a great friend of my mother. Lady Penworthy, this is my daughter, Lady Catriona."

"A great pleasure, Lady Penworthy." Catriona gave a polite curtsey and smiled.

"What a charming young lady! The product of Dumfries's first marriage, of course. You are much too young, Selena, to be the mother of such a grown-up young lady!"

The pretty countess reddened. "Yes, of course. We are more like sisters than mother and daughter. But the word *stepmother* has a rather malevolent connotation, don't you think? Dumfries is so overjoyed to have a family of his own, you know, after so many years of solitude."

Catriona wasn't sure how "solitary" her father had been during his years with the Allied Forces, but it was true he hadn't felt free to marry again until he knew for certain what had become of his first wife, Justine. Her mother.

A brave young woman who dressed as a man so that she could do her part to rescue innocent people condemned to the guillotine. Catriona wished she had been able to know her. She had a feeling Justine would not have been content to live a life of excess and avarice the rest of her life any more than Catriona was.

Selena Hamilton, a great-niece of Sir William Hamilton, had offered to help him with Catriona's transformation from a

Spanish farm girl to a society lady. She'd been twenty-six and on the shelf according to many, but her kind and generous nature had attracted the interest of the much older earl. They'd married only weeks after the signing of the Treaty of Fontainebleau that left Napoleon imprisoned on Elba. Selena had been charmed by Dumfries since she had first met him in her second season, but he had always been too busy with his military activities to pay much attention to the social world.

Until Catriona had come into his life, when the urge to become a family man had finally struck him. And he couldn't have found a more suitable wife. Not at all like the intrepid Justine of his youth, Selena made him feel youthful once more. Had Justine lived, his life would have evolved very differently. But with Selena… his life had become joyful again. Catriona's heart surged with happiness for him.

In some ways, though, Catriona felt out of place. She didn't care if she never saw her adoptive parents again, but she sometimes missed her sisters. And her heart ached for Abuela. Would they ever see each other again? Why did her grandmother never answer her letters? Were Hector and Consuelo keeping them from her out of spite?

And then there was Rupert. Would her heart ever allow her to forget the handsome soldier who'd made such a deep impression on her life?

Or perhaps she should go back to her original thought of becoming a nun. Her father would never allow it, even if there *were* any convents in England. She wondered if her father would consider allowing her to establish a charitable organization—a hospital or a foundling home, perhaps. Something more beneficial to the world than the life of a social butterfly.

Surely God had something more in mind for her than endless

balls and parties.

March 20, 1815
Brussels, Belgium
Townhouse of the Earl of Dumfries

"Bonaparte is in Paris," the earl said when he came down to the breakfast table where Catriona was already sipping her chocolate. "The upstart has already installed himself in the Tuileries, as though he never abdicated at all!"

Catriona raised an eyebrow. "Not so surprising, Papa. We've been expecting it to happen since he escaped from the island." She sighed and shook her head. "More fighting. More casualties. Will it ever end, do you think?"

Her father covered her hand with his. "You will be safe. I've made arrangements for you and Selena and our English servants to return to Surrey the day after tomorrow. Madame Colbert has been given the order to begin packing immediately."

Catriona's cup clattered as it was abruptly dropped from her hand. "I should like to stay, Papa!"

"No, my dear. I cannot allow you to remain here, not with Bonaparte so near and a battle looming. It is impossible."

"I can't leave you alone, Papa!"

"I won't be alone. Madame Colbert and a few of the Belgian servants will be here to cook and clean. In any case, I shall be occupied with March and the rest of the staff. It is said Bonaparte is amassing a huge army and our soldiers are spread far and wide by now. The Allied Forces must focus on strategy if we are to defeat him."

Catriona rose from her chair and strolled over to embrace her father.

"Please let me stay, Papa! I can help! Lady Covington is turning her home into a hospital—there will be so many injured soldiers! Why can't we do that too? This house has more than a dozen rooms that could be turned into hospital wards, and I believe Madame Colbert and the other servants will help!"

Her father pursed his lips. "It is too dangerous, Catriona. And not suitable for a young lady. You should return with your stepmother to London and take your place in the *ton*. Selena assures me that she will be well enough to sponsor you again this year."

She noticed how his manner softened when he spoke of Selena and their coming child. After what had happened the first time when he'd sent off his pregnant wife to safety, he was doubly determined to make sure history would not repeat itself.

She kissed him on the cheek. "Selena will be all right, Papa. The boat will not sink this time. It could not."

He chuckled and patted her hand around his neck. "I suppose your *Diós* told you that."

She smiled and slipped into the chair next to him. "I have faith, yes. This time it will go well with the birth. You will see."

Her father hugged her to him. "I don't know why I believe you, but I do." He kissed the top of her head. "But I did lose your mother, you know. And you as well, for nearly two decades. Allowing you to stay in Brussels when it could become a bloodbath—I don't see how I can possibly do it, my dear."

Catriona looked him directly in the eyes. "You will not lose me again, *papá mía.* I am no fainthearted sheltered young English lady. I shoveled out horse manure. I cooked and cleaned and plowed fields. I learned about healing from Abuela. Blood does not frighten me. Papa," she said, her face devoid of emotion. "I appreciate your wishing to erase the past and replace it with the life you wished for me before I was born, but I can never live my life as nothing but a society lady. I want to do something useful… work with poor people or orphans—or tend to wounded soldiers. That is who I am, Papa. I hope you are not too disappointed."

He smiled. "I could never be disappointed in you, my dear. It is true that I keep trying to over-protect you, as though you are the child I never knew rather than the woman you are." He groaned. "Will I have this much trouble with your sister or brother when it is your age?"

She sat back in the chair. "Of course! I am the older sister and I shall teach him everything I know."

"And I shall be too old to be able to do a thing about it."

He picked up his fork and began to eat his cold breakfast. "I surrender, Catriona. You shall have your hospital. I shall refer you to the Surgeon General for assistance, and make funds available to you in my banking institution here. But you must promise to take a maid with you at all times. I am aware that you have slipped the leash many times since we've been here. But war is a different matter."

Catriona's heart soared. Finally… she would do something more useful than learn to dance the waltz.

The thought of dancing with Rupert came to her quickly and suddenly.

Oh Rupert! Where are you? Will I ever see you again?

Chapter 3

June 12, 1815
Brussels, Belgium
Townhouse of the Earl of Dumfries

"*Pardonnez-moi, mademoiselle,* but Marie tells me she is too ill to serve you today."

Madame Colbert, the Dumfries's Belgian housekeeper, wasn't accustomed to the work of ladies' maid, but then, in times of crisis, one had to make do. And the home she had managed for over a decade—now leased to the Dumfries—no longer resembled the elegant townhouse it had been.

The stylish furnishings had been removed and stored in a warehouse for safekeeping while the larger rooms were fitted with army cots and various sorts of tables and storage closets. Catriona had moved to her stepmother's room in the master suite, and hers, along with several guest bedrooms, were fitted out to be used for sleeping rooms for the round-the-clock staff. The kitchen, while still in the business of serving food, had also become a sort of apothecary's storeroom, with shelves of jars containing medicines, herbs, and other healing substances.

The servants who remained and the volunteers Catriona had managed to round up were all being schooled in basic battlefield medicine by a member of Wellington's own staff of surgeons—

her father's contacts had proved to be most helpful. While a few of the recruits were experienced nurses, none had ever been anywhere near a battlefield, and doctors were few and far between. Catriona had a very real fear that her inexperienced staff might be required to do procedures they were completely unqualified for, such as severing limbs or digging for shrapnel. Which was why she was desperately seeking out surgeons anywhere she could find them.

"I can dress myself, Madame Colbert. I'm to collect some medicines from the apothecary, not attend a ball."

Catriona gave her hair a last brush stroke and pinned it up behind her head. "Hand me that white apron, will you? With my old shawl and bonnet, I shall appear a servant and it won't be remarked upon that I have no maid with me."

Madame Colbert frowned. "But *mademoiselle,* I promised your father…"

"He's gone for the day. I'll only be gone for an hour or so. I can manage on my own, *madame.*"

The housekeeper looked doubtful, but Catriona was mistress of the house in the absence of her father, and she was clearly in a different league from most young ladies of quality. Her father had had to accept that in her, and had more than once told her how much she resembled his Justine… miraculous really since they had grown up in such very different circumstances.

With Napoleon's advance expected at any day, the streets were bustling with pedestrians, horses, carriages, and all sorts of vehicles, as everyone seemed to be stocking up for a battle. The green grocers typically sold out before noon and spent the afternoon traveling far into the countryside to replenish their stock. Butchers, bakers, wine sellers, chandlers—all were toiling harder than they ever had to before to manage the demand. Even the tailors had to hire more seamstresses to supply the endless demand for uniforms for the military men returning to their regiments after months of civilian life.

Catriona reached the apothecary's shop with no problems, her humble clothing having transformed her into just another servant on a commission from her employer.

The apothecary's wife gave her a second look before giving a startled smile. "*Mademoiselle la comtesse,* I almost did not know you in your… disguise."

Catriona explained about her maid, and Madame Roland shook her head disapprovingly before admitting her to the back room of the shop.

"*Très bien, mademoiselle.* I was able to find most of the items on your list, but a few of them, including laudanum, are becoming more difficult to find. *Mon mari* has gone out of town seeking more suppliers, but I can't promise you much more than we've already found for you."

Catriona's face took on a pensive expression. From all she had learned from the army surgeons, laudanum was essential for keeping patients quiet and still during the more painful procedures. Finally, she smiled and accepted the package Madame Roland had prepared for her.

"*Merci, madame.* I shall have to ask the surgeon general for assistance. He has been most helpful thus far."

It was indeed fortunate that her father had so many contacts among the top level officers. They all spoke very highly of Colonel McIntosh, including the Iron Duke himself when she'd met him at a ball. She'd found them all extremely eager to help her in her quest to offer aid to the wounded soldiers in the upcoming battle, even if they *did* question why a young lady with her connections would involve herself in such unpleasant business.

Of course, they didn't know her upbringing. Or about Rupert either.

Even after nearly three years had passed, Catriona recalled those precious few days as clearly as though it were yesterday. What had happened to him? Had he sustained another injury and died? Or even lost his memory as her mother had. He hadn't come back, she was certain, because if so, Abuela would have given him the letter. If she had been able to, that is.

It was also possible that Rupert had changed his mind. The peasant girl Catalina was hardly a suitable marriage prospect for a gentleman in his position, and even now, after her miraculous elevation to the nobility, she had a few black marks against her as a marriage prospect. She shouldn't blame him if he had decided against her, but… she did. Perhaps she was wrong to find every other gentleman wanting in comparison to her Rupert, but in all honesty, that was what she had done. No man could measure up to her memory of Rupert, but their time together had been so short. Perhaps the devotion he'd proclaimed had been nothing but a result of the intimacy they'd shared.

Engrossed in her thoughts, she wasn't watching where she was going and bumped a passer-by on the pavement. Concern for the safety of the parcel that slipped out of her arms, she didn't notice the gentleman she'd run into until he deftly caught it and turned to hand it back to her.

"Oh, thank you, *monsieur,*" she began, "I feared the glass bottles would break—"

And then they looked at each other and froze.

It was Rupert.

Catalina felt disoriented and would have dropped the parcel again had not Rupert—or should she address him as Mr.

Ellsworth now that she knew he was not dead and had obviously abandoned her?—caught her arm.

"Catalina! Bloody hell! What are you doing *here?*"

~

Rupert was astounded. It couldn't be Catalina… and yet it was features he recognized under the faded black bonnet. That same embroidered gray shawl. He closed his eyes and opened them again.

He wasn't imagining it. He'd been thinking of Catalina a great deal since his return to England and his father's determination to marry him off to some brainless English chit. He'd not found any woman equal to Catalina in character or courage, and he'd found it difficult to accept anything less than a woman who could be a true partner—his other half. And when he'd finally given up the search and answered Wellington's call to arms—against his father's wishes—here she was, alive! In Brussels, of all places!

For an instant he saw a light in her eyes that indicated relief and welcome. But her expression quickly became more distant. She backed away, clutching her parcel to her chest.

"Rupert. You look… well."

Her command of his language had improved considerably, but he missed the adorable trilling of the R in Rupert. Where had she been? How had she come all the way from Spain to Belgium? Why had her family insisted she was dead? He recalled the coldness that had gripped his soul upon seeing the gravestone with her name on it.

He reached out to touch her arm, but she backed away. Why the cold greeting? Had she married another in his absence? A soldier who had brought her here, to the site of the ultimate contest between Bonaparte and the Iron Duke?

"We must talk, Catalina." He scanned the busy street. "What about the *pâtisserie* on the corner? May I buy you a tart?"

She gave a furtive look down the street and continued to retreat. "No! That is, I'm sorry, Mr. Ellsworth, but I cannot stop now. I-I am expected elsewhere." She forced a smile. "I am pleased to see you so well recovered from your injury."

She turned away to depart. "I must go. Please—take care."

He thought her voice broke as she almost broke into a run in her eagerness to leave him.

What was this? She wouldn't even *talk* to him? After the promises they'd made to each other? He'd grieved for her once when he'd thought her lost to him forever, but now that he knew she lived still and apparently no longer cared for him… that stung him to his very soul.

Then he straightened up and began following her in her distinctive gray shawl. She bloody hell did owe him an explanation—even if she didn't care for him anymore.

She continued her progress several more blocks with him keeping a safe distance away. A few times she glanced behind her as if expecting pursuit, but Rupert had learned the trick of becoming invisible through his service as an explorer scout, and she never saw him.

Eventually, she opened a gate and approached the door of a townhouse and was welcomed inside by a middle-aged woman who looked to be a servant.

Rupert stood on the corner and stroked his chin. The townhouse she'd entered was situated in a very upscale neighborhood, not the sort of place where a common soldier would live with his wife. And she wasn't dressed in the manner of a lady who lived in such a place. Could she be a servant? But a servant wouldn't enter by the front door, would she?

As much as he wanted to knock on the door and demand an explanation, he reluctantly decided to leave it to another day. He knew her address; he would make inquiries among his fellow officers and let that determine his next course of action.

Catalina was alive!

June 13, 1817
Brussels, Belgium
Office of the Earl of March

"His Grace expects Boney to attack from the west, but as someone who's fought the sly little Frog before, I'd wager a monkey he'll attack from the east just to throw the allies in disarray."

Charles Gordon-Lennox, the Earl of March and eldest son of the Duke of Richmond, paced back and forth between the twin windows behind his desk. A couple of decades younger than the Iron Duke, he was several inches taller and was everything a soldier could wish for in a commander. He'd served with Wellington in the Peninsula as aide-de-camp and Rupert knew him to be a man of integrity, cool and level-headed, with a good grasp of military strategy.

Rupert shook his head. "Can't take you up on it. Happens I agree with you. But we've already got scouts keeping eyes on them. No doubt the duke has an alternate plan in mind."

March paused, seemingly staring out of the window.

"Damned if I know why he palmed me off as aide-de-camp to that boy-prince! Thinks he's a goddamned military genius because he's studied military history. Book knowledge! Bah!"

Rupert privately agreed with his comrade, but the "boy"—Slender Billy as he was nicknamed—did have military experience in the Peninsula and had been, in fact, Wellington's aide-de-camp at one time. Still, there was no doubt that March was considerably more qualified for command. But he wasn't a prince, for all that.

"Suppose it makes sense to have a Dutch commander over a Dutch-Belgian brigade."

"Bah! We both know he did it because the Dutch insisted on it as a price for their participation. His Grace—"

"Is that Lady Catriona down there with Sir James? Wonder what she could want with the Medical Corps?"

Rupert moved forward. "Lady Catriona? I don't believe I've met—"

His eyes focused on a dark-haired lady in a bottle green *à la hussar* pelisse with gold trim. For a moment she turned her face in his direction, and he realized with a jolt that it was Catalina.

He felt giddy. What? Was she now impersonating a lady? The Catalina he knew would never…

March clapped a hand on his shoulder. "Quite a stunner, ain't she? Dumfries' long-lost daughter. Appeared on the London scene last summer and took the *ton* by storm." He shook his head. "A beauty and an heiress. Be married long ago if she weren't a papist. By God, I'd have married her myself if not for that. The Pater won't stand for it. The next Duke of Richmond can't sire a line of little papists."

"Dumfries' *daughter?*" Colonel McIntosh had been his commander back in the latter months of 1811 when he'd first joined the army. In fact, he had been such during the summer he and Catalina had met… until a few weeks later when he'd returned to England due to family exigency.

Family exigency? Catalina—Catriona? It didn't make sense.

But he *would* get to the bottom of it.

He made his excuses to his astonished comrade and raced to

the door.

~

"Thank you most kindly, Sir James, on behalf of my father and myself, our staff of volunteers, and certainly the injured who come our way."

The Director-General of the Army Medical Department reached for her hand and kissed it. "The shoe is on the other foot, my lady. It's lassies as compassionate as ye that remind our brave men why they are fighting this wretched war."

Catriona curtsied and took her leave. Her maid coughed hoarsely and Catriona bit her lip.

"You are still unwell, Marie! What was I thinking to pull you out of bed before you have recovered?"

It was a rhetorical question. Catriona could not have called upon Sir James McGrigor dressed as a maid and unescorted, and Marie was the only person who could be spared.

"*Je suis bien*," Marie insisted. "It sounds worse than it is, *croyez-moi.*"

"Nevertheless, you will go right back to bed as soon as we return."

The carriage pulled up and Catriona was about to put her foot on the step when a hand was offered. Believing it to be the coachman, she began, "No need, *monsieur*. I can manage on my—"

Words failed her when she glanced at the face of the man to whom the hand belonged. *Rupert?*

The expression on his face was shuttered and distant. "I presume I'm addressing Lady Catriona? Today, at least."

Catriona shivered. From discomfort or… something else. From his nearness? Her throat went dry.

"Rupert… "

He pointed his head toward the carriage. "We need to talk, you and I. Shall I accompany you to your home?"

Catriona swallowed. "Er-yes. All right. I suppose—"

"I'll ride *dessus* with the coachman," Marie offered.

"But you're ill. Here… take my pelisse. It'll keep you warm enough."

Marie pulled the beautiful green garment over her shoulders. *"Merci, mademoiselle. C'est si belle."*

Although it was a warm day, Catriona shivered as she arranged herself in the forward-facing seat. Her lemon yellow day gown sported a more modest neckline than her ball gowns, but low décolletages—scandalously low, in her opinion—were in fashion and it was clear that Rupert noticed her cleavage.

How could he not? All men did, and some were uncouth enough to speak to her chest instead of her face.

Not Rupert, though. Once the wheels began to turn, he demanded an explanation.

Her eyes narrowed. "I don't owe you any explanations, Mr. Ellsworth."

His eyes widened. "Do you not, Señorita Ordóñez? When last we met, you were a sweet young thing who was thinking of joining a convent, and now I find you impersonating an earl's daughter." He sneered. "And doing a fine job of it too. Apparently you have deceived the whole of London society, as well as the Earl of Dumfries."

He leaned forward and grabbed her shoulders. "Tell me, were you ever really young and sweet? Or was *that* a disguise as well?" His mouth slanted over hers and his kiss was harsh, punishing.

Catriona pushed him back and slapped him, her eyes throwing sparks. "How dare you? I have done nothing wrong!

You are the one who made promises he couldn't keep!"

Her vision blurred through sudden tears as she recalled the weeks and months of waiting and worrying that he might have been killed… or that he had had second thoughts about his promise to come for her.

Rupert's head jerked back. "What do you mean? I kept *my* promise! I came back in December just before I was called home. But you weren't there. You were dead, they told me!"

Now it was Catriona's turn to be incredulous. "Dead? But-but–did not Abuela show you my letter? She promised she would give it to you—if you ever came back for me."

Rupert stiffened. "Catalina—" He took her hand in his and squeezed it.

The color drained out of her face. "What is it? Tell me, Rupert!"

But she knew even before his words confirmed it. The reason he'd never received her letter. The reason Abuela had never answered her letters. Abuela had been ill prior to her departure. She'd never recovered. Her beloved grandmother was dead.

Catriona collapsed against the squabs, and other than being carried into the house in Rupert's capable arms, she couldn't remember the remainder of that carriage ride.

Except… had he kissed her? Lightly this time, on the top of her head after laying her down gently on her bed. However, knowing how angry he was with her, she must have dreamed it.

Chapter 4

June 14, 1815
Brussels, Belgium
Office of Colonel Tobias McIntosh, Earl of Dumfries

Rupert paced anxiously outside the door of the earl's office, his dress uniform spotless and wrinkle-free, his buttons polished to a burnished gold and his best Hoby boots shiny from a liberal application of saliva, which his father's valet insisted was more efficacious than the champagne favored by Brummell.

He'd taken great care with his appearance that morning—all done by himself since he had no valet here—because it was his intention to ask the colonel for his daughter's hand in marriage.

Because one glance at the anguish in Catalina's—no Catriona's—eyes and he knew she was no adventuress. He didn't know how or why, but she *was* the earl's long-lost daughter. Incredible though it seemed, she was telling the truth… he saw it in her eyes. And what he also saw there gave him grounds to hope that she still cared for him.

He knew he'd have to grovel. And that she might suspect him of being a fortune hunter. But he'd do whatever he could to win her.

He stopped pacing in front of the door and hit the side of his head with his palm. How lucky could he be? He'd thought her dead these past years, grieved for her, found fault with all the other ladies his father put in his path, and now… she was alive! Vibrant and beautiful and the object of other men's lust. His fists clenched at the memory of March's expression of desire for her. She was his, damn it, and other men could keep their eyes to themselves!

"Something bothering you, Ellsworth? No need to punch a hole in the door. I'll be glad to open it for you first."

His commander—then and now, since they'd both returned to service—clapped him on the shoulder and guided him into the office, which was about as disordered as it could be, with boxes of papers littering just about every available space. Dumfries cleared a chair for him and indicated for him to sit.

"Pardon the chaos, but the staff is relocating to the new quarters in Waterloo. Not much more than a wee hamlet, really, but we must be closer to the action, and that's where Nosey thinks it'll be."

He settled in another facing Rupert, and sat back. "You're in fine feathers today. Expecting a parade?"

Rupert looked the Colonel directly in the eyes—eyes colored the same remarkable blue as Catalina's, he noticed.

"I'm here to request your daughter's hand in marriage."

June 15, 1815
Brussels, Belgium
Townhouse of the Earl of Dumfries

"I don't know why my father insists on my attending this ball," Catriona grumbled as her maid labored over her hair. "I agreed to accompany him when said His Grace ordered all of his officers to attend, but when he was called away, I assumed my own presence would be unnecessary."

"Most *mesdemoiselles* would be *enchantées* at the opportunity to attend such a ball!" exclaimed Marie as she scrutinized her mistress's coiffure for any obvious flaws.

"I'm not *most* young ladies, as you surely know by now, Marie. With Bonaparte heading this way and an imminent confrontation about to occur, I simply cannot understand anyone—let alone the duke himself—thinking it appropriate to have a ball at this time!"

She rose from the dressing table and waved a piece of paper in her maid's face. "There are so many things I could be doing to better prepare for a houseful of wounded soldiers. Dancing and exchanging banalities with overdressed *aristos* are not on the list!"

Marie snatched the list out of Catriona's hands and replaced it

to

she

ess,

sse!

an

uld

iful

by

en.

sn't

ine

ain

ow

angry he'd been when he'd believed her an impostor. She'd been wounded by his hasty misconception, but he'd had good reason to be suspicious, given the circumstances.

A carriage—her father's, she saw as she glanced out of the window—pulled up to the gate, and a uniformed officer descended from carriage. The soldier's sizable crested helmet obscured his face, and she wondered idly which of his subalterns her father had assigned to escort her. Older or younger? Married or unattached? It didn't really matter. It was just another ball, after all. She forced a smile and made her way to the stairs.

From his position in the foyer, Rupert waited anxiously for Catalina—that was, Lady Catriona—to appear. Would she refuse to accompany him when she became aware of the identity of her escort? He couldn't blame her if she did—he should have had enough sense to know that she was too honorable for the deception he'd accused her of. Even so, he was already strategizing alternate means of winning her. Because she was his!

When Lady Catriona appeared at the top of the stairs, Rupert's mouth dropped open. A vision in blue—the exact marine blue of her eyes—with rich gold trim and a tiara sparkling with diamonds, she was every bit the countess. For a brief moment, he wondered if the Catalina he loved was still there, but then she smiled at him with Catalina's smile and his doubts fled.

"Rupert!"

There was moment of surprise when her gloved fingers flew to her throat, but she didn't try to hide the pleasure she felt at seeing him.

"Lady Catriona."

"So… you know."

"I saw your father."

By this time, she had reached the hall and he made her an elegant bow and kissed her hand.

She was trembling with excitement. "I'm sorry. I wanted to tell you—"

He put a gloved index finger against her lips. "Not tonight, my love. This evening is for *us.*"

Her eyes sparkled and she appeared to relax.

He took the blue cloak the butler handed him and draped it carefully around her shoulders before fastening the hooks slowly so that he could admire her face. The darling turned-up nose and rose-red lips, both of which he yearned to kiss, the tawny-beige complexion he already knew was soft to the touch. She was a perfect, exotic creature. And she was his.

Kissing distance apart, he gazed directly into her eyes.

"You are the most beautiful creature I have ever beheld, my lady."

She smiled but did not look away. "You are quite the most handsome gentleman yourself, Mr. Ellsworth."

They stood there, their hearts in their eyes, for several long moments until the butler's discreet cough brought them back to the present.

Rupert held out his arm. "Your carriage awaits, my lady."

She accepted his arm. "My father's carriage, you mean."

"Indeed. A very obliging gentleman, your father."

The coachman put out the iron steps and Rupert gave his arm to assist her into the carriage.

"Was this your idea or his?" she asked when they settled into their seats.

"He devised the scheme when I confided my desire to win your hand in marriage."

Her eyes widened.

"Don't say anything. I haven't asked you yet," he said with a grin. "We still have a ball to attend."

The old coach-house on the rue de Blanchisserie had been transformed into an elegant ballroom, with rose-trellises printed on the wallpaper, elaborate chandeliers, and sumptuous hangings of crimson, gold and black. Even more impressive, however, were the colorful uniforms of the dignitaries in attendance, foremost of all, the Prince of Orange, whose blue and orange uniform had an explosion of colored medals across the chest and an orange cockade in his helmet. "Slender Billy" took one look at Catriona and started in their direction, but Rupert steered her away quickly, seeing with relief that the "boy prince" had been waylaid by the Duchess of Richmond.

A waltz began to play. He bowed. "May I have this dance, Lady Catriona?"

She nodded and held out her arms. They circled the floor, eyes so intent on each other that the guests began to whisper.

"A most handsome couple, don't you think?"

"Is that Ellsworth's heir?"

"Does he know she's a papist? Don't reckon that father of his will ever approve."

"Lucky bloke!" This last came from Charles Gordon-Lennox, Earl of March, who knew his mother would make a scene—yes, even at her own ball—if he should so much as *dance* with Lady Catriona.

As much as he wished to, Rupert couldn't monopolize her presence the entire evening. She danced with Captain Widman, aide-de-camp to the Earl of Uxbridge, Wellington's second in command, and several eager youths, officers and civilians alike. Each time, however, Rupert came to collect her, leaving no doubts that she belonged to him.

He didn't have to worry too much about the Prince of Orange. Almost as soon as the duke himself arrived, Slender Billy was called over and ordered to leave, which seemed to irk him greatly as supper had not even been served yet.

This incident gave Rupert more to think about than the blessed absence of the boy prince. Something was happening behind the scenes. Wellington and some of his officers disappeared for awhile, and when they returned, little by little, more and more officers began to slip away. A grim-faced duke danced with Lady Georgiana Gordon-Lennox, the daughter of the host, and afterward, when she rushed out of the ballroom in tears, the rumors spread like wildfire.

"A skirmish at Quatre-Bras!"

"Boney is headed this way as we speak."

"They say he has twenty thousand troops."

"The Grande-Armée? Oh no, at least a hundred thousand, my dear. Frightening, really, when you consider that our forces aren't even fully assembled yet."

"My son is so eager to go into battle and return a hero. With all those bullets flying, I shan't sleep a minute until I know he's come back safe."

Rupert's turn came when a footman brought him a hastily scrawled note from the duke and he hurried to the duke's side.

"You're to accompany Dumfries to the area around Quatre-Bras. Midnight. He has your orders." The duke waved a hand in the direction of Catriona, who was chatting nearby with an older lady dressed in the fashion of two decades earlier.

"Couldn't help but notice your interest in Dumfries' daughter. Lovely gel, that. Papist, you know. Such a pity! Can't marry a Catholic and sit in Parliament, you know."

Rupert ground his teeth to tamp down his irritation. "I fully approve of Lady Catriona's devotion to her faith. She saved my life, Your Grace, and I'd not hesitate to put it into her hands again, if necessary."

"Well, well," the Duke said, stroking his chin. "You've got it bad, Ellsworth. But if it means anything, I think you're a lucky man. Damned lucky."

Rupert saluted and pulled out his pocket watch. Almost eleven! He had to find some way to sweep his ladylove away for a proposal before duty called him to the battlefield.

~

The *baronne* leaned across the table and whispered loudly in the direction of Catriona's ear. *"Un bel homme, sans doute,* your young man," she confided.

Catriona was certain the older ladies at the next table had ceased their chatter in order to eavesdrop on their conversation.

"Has he money or property?"

Catriona shrugged. She didn't know or care.

"A title, *au moins.*"

"No."

The *baronne* leaned back and threw up her hands. "In that case, *ma chère,* you would be much better with Marchand's heir. No money, *naturellement,* but he will have a title—sooner than later—his father drinks too much—and he comes from a family that serves the True Church."

Catriona wanted to tell the meddling old lady in no uncertain terms what she thought of her suggestions, but decided against it.

"Candidly, *madame la baronne,* those things are of no importance to me. I have known poverty in my life before"—here the *baronne's* eyes widened, since Catriona's upbringing had not been made public—"and it does not frighten me. Money, titles—if I should lose them all today, it would not be the end of the world for me, as long as I can be with a man who loves me enough to value me as an equal partner."

The *baronne* peered at her through her quizzing glass. "And you believe Monsieur Ellsworth is that man?"

Catriona smiled. "I love him."

The *baronne* was speechless, perhaps for the first time in her life.

That was when Rupert approached them.

"Bon soir, madame," he said with a nod at the *baronne.* "Lady Catriona, will you accompany me to the terrace? An urgent matter has arisen and I must speak to you."

He led her—pulled, more like, Catriona thought—toward the terrace. On any other night, such behavior would be scandalous in the extreme, but on that particular night, with officers leaving left and right and anxious ladies dabbing at their eyes at the prospect of a dreadful battle, nobody seemed to notice.

The first thing he did when they were finally alone was pull her against him and kiss her passionately. Urgently. Like a man who was going off to war, she thought bemusedly as she eagerly responded.

"I heard what you said," he blurted out when the kiss ended. "To the old lady. I love you too, Catriona."

He gave her a sheepish look. "This wasn't how I planned it. I promise I'll do it all again properly, once the war is over. But I couldn't go off to battle without asking you to marry me." He looked at her anxiously. "I say, you will, won't you? Your father gave me his permission—and this ring that belonged to your mother"—he fumbled to find it in his pocket and placed it on her left hand. "You'll have my family betrothal ring when we return to Surrey."

She gazed at the ring and giggled. "This is my mother's ring—the one he already gave me before he apparently took it back. But it's a perfect betrothal ring, Rupert. And a most—er—interesting proposal. I would love to be your wife."

Rupert gave a yelp of joy and they were in other's arms.

They pretended not to hear the sound of horses' hooves and carriage wheels in the street, not wanting to part, but finally Rupert pulled away.

"It's time," he said. "I'm to meet your father at your home at midnight. Apparently there was a bit of a scuffle at Quatre Bras today."

"Rupert," she said before they returned to the ballroom, "please stay on your horse this time. And away from those dreadful French bullets."

Chapter 5

June 16-18, 1815
Brussels, Belgium
Townhouse of the Earl of Dumfries

The carts of wounded sent by the Army Medical Department began rolling in the following day, at first sporadically, with a handful of soldiers injured in the skirmishes between the two sides, and then, by late afternoon, in larger numbers as the battle to control the crossroads at Quatre Bras intensified. Other than scanning each soldier's face for reassurance that neither Rupert nor her father were among them, Catriona and her mostly-inexperienced staff were too busy to dwell on their own personal concerns.

Of course, hers wasn't the only hospital in the city, and the dead—when they could be safely retrieved—were housed elsewhere. She tried to concentrate on assisting the physicians—who divided their time between several hospitals—and treating wounds. She quickly learned to put on a cheerful face and give the appearance of confidence even though she was aghast at some of the procedures she was called upon to do. Not one to be fazed by the sight of blood, she learned to stitch wounds—even head wounds, like Rupert's—by observing the physicians at work. Thereafter, she routinely did such procedures herself, expedience being more important than skill.

As the hours passed, however, and the number of casualties increased exponentially, the physicians became few and far between. More homes became temporary hospitals, but even so, wounded soldiers lined the streets. Volunteer nurses ranged from delicate ladies who could do little but tear up cloth for bandages and plain folk and servants who were rather more helpful. Catriona found herself doing procedures she never expected to do, such as prod human flesh for bullets and set broken bones. She set her limit at amputations, but knew that if it meant saving a life, she'd manage to do that as well.

Rumors of the progress of the war were rampant. Blücher's army was defeated by the French the first day and had to retreat. The French troops were fresh, trained and devoted to their *empereur*. Wellington's army was a ragtag band of soldiers of various nationalities, most of whom were inexperienced, and some—most of the Belgians—with divided loyalties wore their old uniforms of the Grande Armée they had served with in the past.

The third day was the worst. Massive numbers of wounded were brought to hospitals, many expiring before they arrived. Catriona and her staff had soldiers everywhere, including the master suite and the floors. Supplies were becoming depleted, to the point where Catriona began tearing up curtains and even her own gowns for bandages. Laudanum was impossible to find, so she ordered them to use it sparingly, raiding her father's stash of brandy instead.

Rumors abounded that the number of the dead was enormous, and that most of the fallen still lay in the valley, open to scavenging Belgians who picked their pockets and even dug their teeth out of their mouths. Catriona slept little and prayed much, often falling asleep in front of her make-shift altar, rosary in hand.

She begged God to keep them safe, and yet she knew that His ways were not hers. Even Sor Juana, with all of her highly ranked supporters, had been forced to stop writing and studying when the Archbishop of Mexico had confiscated her books, destroyed most of her writings and ordered her to do penance for her great sin in defending the role of women.

Catriona did not blame God for that, however. The True Church that she adhered to was not made of oppressors who sought to use God as justification for their heartless depravity. The True Church was not contained in a building, and focused its efforts on serving the poor and downtrodden, as Jesus Christ did during his sojourn on earth. She herself was and would always be a devout Catholic, but she believed the True Church enveloped all true believers, regardless of creed or sect. It wasn't up to her or any other human to determine the state of another's soul—only God was capable of determining that. Anything else was simply unimportant.

On the third day, the question in everyone's mind seemed to be: When were the Prussians coming? The fighting was intense and neither side seemed to be dominating, bad news and good news often arriving at the same time.

It all seemed to depend on Blücher and his Prussians. Where were they?

June 16, 1815
Allied Headquarters
Waterloo, Belgium

"Ellsworth, you'll go east and keep me informed of Blücher's progress. If Boney's allowed to drive a wedge between us, we'll have to face his *Grande Armée* without him. I'll divert some Allied troops his way when I can."

The Iron Duke turned to the older man.

"Dumfries, you're to patrol the western flank. You'll report to me, directly, but see if you can't knock some sense into Slender Billy. Can't trust a man whose ambition outweighs his loyalty."

The earl bowed his head, but Rupert could see he wasn't best pleased. All the earl's experience in tact and diplomacy would most likely be useless when pitted against the arrogance and vanity of the Dutch prince.

Dismissed, the two men paused outside the door. It was barely dawn and neither had slept or eaten, although they had taken the time to change out of their dress uniforms and don their battle gear before heading out to the battleground, unlike some they'd seen in the street.

The earl clapped a hand on Rupert's shoulder. "Take care of yourself, Ellsworth. I suspect you're my only hope of getting grandchildren any time soon."

"Likewise," Rupert said, extending his arm for a handshake. "I should dislike in the extreme returning to Lady Catriona without you, sir."

The two men parted and from then on, Rupert tried to keep his mind and senses focused on his assignment. It was more difficult to do than he expected, however. While every soldier has an innate instinct for self-preservation, it seemed to be more potent this time, now that he had Catriona waiting for him, depending on him—well, no, not really. His betrothed depended on no man. She had known hardship before and survived, and she would do so again, as many times as necessary. Many men would not like that quality in a woman, preferring to be the strong one, the dominant one whose word was law. His father had been such a one, demanding that his wife submit to his authority, without any consideration for her or their family, and that was how he'd lost her.

And if he should try the same tacts with Rupert in the matter of his marriage to a Catholic, he'd lose his only remaining son as well. Because Rupert would no longer be dictated to by tyrants. The miracle of finding and falling in love with Catriona had removed his father's power over him. From that point on, he was a man unto himself. Whatever the future held, he had no fear of it. Catriona's faith and courage were now his as well.

The news he brought from the Prussians was calamitous. Napoleon's twenty thousand troops were decimating Blücher's forces, and the Allied forces, desperately attempting to keep the French from taking Quatre-Bras, the crossroads that gave a strategic advantage to the army that controlled it, were unable to lend support. The Prussians lost that day, and on the next, the Allied army was forced to retreat north, further still from their Prussian allies.

In the end, Boney's army won no territory that day, but Rupert didn't hear any of the top brass calling it a victory. Too many deaths. Too many blunders.

Scots infantry shooting at the Dutch Prince's retreating cavalry, taking their blue uniforms for French ones.

Belgian troops—many of whom had fought in the *Grande Armée* and were deathly afraid to fight against it—running for cover instead of fighting.

Rupert personally watched Napoleon's armed cavalry, the *cuirassiers,* slaughter a large part of the 5th Brigade, briefly reaching the crossroads before being driven back by Allied artillery. He personally saw hundreds—maybe thousands—die horrible deaths that day, and, as exhausted as he was after the horrific sights and lack of sleep from the previous night, he slept only fitfully, his mind not allowing him to forget the sights and sounds of men in the throes of death.

June 17, 1815

Rupert reported that Bülow's IV Corps, not having been engaged at Ligny, was fresh and in a good position near Wavre.

A powerful wind in late afternoon heralded the arrival of a storm, the intensity of which Rupert had never seen before. The prematurely dark skies and the deafening thunder hovering over the battlefield seemed to Rupert like divine intervention, but when the deluge of rain poured down in droves and thoroughly soaked him and everyone else who hadn't found shelter immediately, he began to wonder if it was more a judgment than an intervention.

That night he slept like a dead man, taking shelter under a supply wagon with two other men.

June 18, 1815

By the time he awoke, the rain had stopped, leaving a mist over the Mont-St. Jean battlefield. Rupert managed to get down a cup of hot tea before the duke ordered him to Wavre, to find out when to expect the Prussians to march.

The road was so water-logged that for much of the distance his horse's hooves sank three inches into the ground, forcing him to pick his way carefully to avoid a fall. If the road is this bad for one horseman, Rupert thought grimly, how on God's earth could an entire army manage it?

Still, the effects of the torrents of rain would hamper the enemy just as much. He urged his horse on, keeping an eye out for stray bullets, knowing that the French scouts would be milling around as well.

While Blücher assured Rupert that General Bülow's IV Corps would be rounded up directly to march to Wellington's aid, there was something about Bülow's chief of staff's utter tranquility that concerned him. After acknowledging his superior's order and watching him depart, Gneisenau sat down and continued eating his breakfast as though he had all the time in the world.

Rupert, suspecting something fishy was about, remounted his horse and set off toward the west, but once he'd reached a ridge with a clump of trees, he dismounted, climbed one of them, and took out his spyglass to watch the activities of the Prussian camp he had just left.

For the first hour, he couldn't make out anything happening at all. Then, finally, he began to see tents being rolled up and wagons packed. Perhaps they were waiting for the mud to dry a bit before they marched, he thought. Not hearing any battle sounds from the west, he assumed the rest of the army combatants were doing the same.

He dropped out of the tree and followed them at a discreet distance, surprised to see that they were not taking the same route he had—which was obviously the most direct one. Did they know something he did not? Bloody hell, they were taking the army of thirty thousand men through the village of Wavre's narrow streets! Rupert knew from his scouting the previous day that there was a rickety bridge to be traversed further down the road, and he suspected the Prussian leaders were deliberately delaying their arrival.

The Iron Duke had better have a miracle up his sleeve,

Rupert thought as he raced back to Wellington's camp as fast as the road would let him. Because it appeared that he would be facing Napoleon's *Grande Armée* without much help from the Prussians.

He was halfway there when he heard the unmistakable sound of *La marseillaise*, followed by three shots, and he knew the battle was on. He was so focused on getting to Wellington that for a moment he forgot to watch for enemy scouts, and that's when he heard a bullet fly past his ear. His horse reared, but he managed to stay on, in doing so catching sight of a pair of French soldiers coming toward him from the south. Without time to load his rifle and his pistol only useful for short distances, he quickly got the horse under control and urged him toward a wooded area.

If they were searching for Prussians, they were looking in the wrong place, he thought bitterly. He hopped to the ground, gave his horse a slap on the rear, and looked around for a tree to hide behind.

The enemy soldiers slowed as they reached the wood, and hearing the sound of the horse's hooves, took off in that direction. Rupert followed after them, dodging from tree to tree, careful to keep out of sight. Shots rang out and he heard the squeal of his horse as it was plugged with bullets. He had to make his move now, before they discovered the horse was riderless. He aimed his rifle at the soldier closest to him and fired, the bullet hitting the man in the back of the head and dropping him to the ground. While the remaining one whirled around to investigate, Rupert took cover behind a clump of trees, firing a shot in his direction. Rupert heard a cry of pain and the sound of a man dropping to the ground, but still he waited. Detecting no movement from the fallen soldiers, he crept toward them to investigate.

For the second time that day, he heard the sound of a musket firing at him, and this time he felt the bullet pierce the skin of his left arm. Ignoring the blood pouring down his arm, he threw his rifle down and reached for his pistol. As soon as he had the enemy in sight, he pulled the trigger and the young Frenchman, his chest spurting blood, fell to the ground for the last time.

It was only then that he felt the pain of his own wound and became aware of his blood loss. Somehow he managed to tear off what remained of his sleeve and use it to stem the flow of blood. For a brief moment, he rested against the trunk of a nearby tree to get back his bearings. The sounds of the fierce battle taking place to his west and south finally stirred him to action. He made his way on wobbly legs to the downed soldiers and gave them each a kick.

"Damned Frogs," he said. "You've made me break my promise to my beloved. And ruined my jacket too."

With his own horse dead on the ground, he mounted one of the fallen soldiers' mounts and raced to the Allied camp.

Riding an unfamiliar horse virtually one-handed wasn't the easiest thing, he discovered. But he knew the gunshots could easily have been heard by other enemy soldiers, and he had to get away from there before their comrades came to investigate. Somehow he managed to get to Wellington's encampment, where two soldiers helped him off the horse and escorted him to the elm tree where the great man was conferring with several men, one of which, Rupert recognized as the Earl of Dumfries.

"You're injured!" the earl exclaimed as he glimpsed Rupert's arm. "Did you fall off your horse again?"

Rupert tried to smile, but winced instead, as the pain worsened. "I have bad news, Your Grace."

Wellington glared at him. "Blücher's not coming."

"No. That is, he *is*, but… well… he's taking his time."

Rupert reported what he had seen, and the duke swore.

"Don't mind him," the earl whispered. "He's had nothing but bad news today. I just had to tell him that Slender Billy's bloody idiocy caused the deaths of hundreds of good men this day."

Aloud: "With your permission, Your Grace, I'll see this young man to the surgeons' tent."

Once they were out of hearing, the earl shook his head and said in a matter-of-fact voice, "They'd better damned well save the arm, because I'm not sending a one-armed man back to wed my daughter. She'd never forgive me."

Rupert didn't remember much of what happened after that. Before the surgeon arrived to dig the bullet out of his arm, he was given a dose of laudanum that made everything after that seem like a blur. By the time he was conscious again, it was dark and he was being loaded on a wagon bound for Brussels.

The battle had been won. Napoleon was retreating to Paris. But as the duke was quoted later as saying, "It was the nearest-run thing you ever saw in your life."

Epilogue

September 23, 1815
Cranley, Surrey
Ellsworth Manor

"Was the wedding all you wished for, Mrs. Ellsworth? Or should I address you as Lady Catriona? Or even better—*madame la comtesse?* There are just so many choices. No one lady should have so many names!"

Rupert clapped his hand against the side of his head and looked at her in mock confusion.

Catriona, one hand on her delicate lace veil to keep it from blowing off in the strong breeze that had come on just as they arrived at the wedding breakfast on Ellsworth Manor's front lawn, had other concerns.

"Do you see Marie anywhere? I wonder if she might pin down my gown before this wind reveals something scandalous to the guests."

At that point his question finally clicked in her head and she turned to her new husband and smiled coquettishly. "It was a lovely wedding. And you may call me anything you wish, Mr. Ellsworth, so long as you don't call me late for dinner."

Her father by marriage, seated at the head of the table, pursed his lips. "She got that from me!" he protested. "I say that all the time, do I not, Dumfries?"

The earl, at the other end of the table, with his wife on his right, raised an eyebrow. "That's my Cat. Quick learner, she is. The Prince Regent says her English is faultless."

"Well, I said it first," grumbled Rupert's father, crossing his arms across his chest. A footman appeared with a tray of roast beef, and his eyes glazed over. "Fine English roast beef. So delightful."

Catriona narrowed her eyes. "Now Mr. Ellsworth—no, Papa-in-law, I suppose—you know what Dr. Finney said about avoiding beef. Your gout, you know."

Her father-in-law scowled at her. "So now you're the eyes of the good doctor, are you? A traitor in my own home!" He took a tentative bite and chewed it carefully. "I should have thought you'd have had enough of doctoring in Belgium," he muttered.

Her own father winked. "I see you've taken my advice and begun as you mean to go on," he said, leaning over the table toward Catriona.

Her eyes danced. "Oh, he's a pussycat, really. Of course, he wasn't best pleased to be presented with a Papist daughter-in-law who wasn't even born in England, but he's much easier to manage than Rupert led me to believe. I shall have to give my husband lessons."

"Darling," said Rupert, catching her hand under the table. "Say my name the way you did in Spain. You know, R-Rupert. It sounds so—romantic."

The earl snorted and grinned at his wife. "Now, now, save that for the wedding night."

The older Ellsworth agreed. "Indeed. We don't want people thinking my daughter-in-law can't speak the King's English properly."

"When can we get out of here?" Rupert whispered in Catriona's ear.

Catriona sighed. "Not for awhile yet. Not until the guests have all been served, at least."

And there were a lot of them. Rupert's father had insisted upon inviting the entire village of Cranley, as well as his own tenants, and many of Dumfries's friends and servants had made the trip over from Cambridgeshire. It seemed everyone wanted to meet Rupert's new bride and eventual viscountess… although she already had titles of her own.

Catriona, eager to meet the locals of the area where she would be living, was already making plans to establish a small hospital staffed with a trained physician and nurses. And then someone had mentioned the woeful inadequacy of the local school. Frankly, she had been too busy with important projects to be much involved in planning her own wedding, so she'd left it to the capable hands of her stepmother, Selena.

"There is so much food," she observed, as empty platters were quickly replaced. "This lot would have fed the entire village of Las Torres for months!"

"My wife, the philanthropist," Rupert said fondly as he stroked the small of her back. "I've already given instructions for the leftovers to be packed up and distributed to the parish poor. The vicar's wife was eager to take on the project."

"Well… I suppose that will do." But his bride looked disappointed.

Rupert's arm slipped around her waist slowly and deliberately. "We have other important matters to undertake tonight, my love."

His fingers lightly touched the underside of her breast, and she trembled.

"Indeed," she whispered. "I haven't forgotten. In fact, I'm quite looking forward to it. It's just that—"

"—you like to organize things," finished Rupert, whose eyes were focused on Catriona's moist red lips. "For once in your life, *ma chère*, trust me to manage this particular undertaking."

Catriona fluttered her eyelashes. "Well, perhaps this once, R-Rupert dear, but you mustn't expect it ever after."

Rupert's eyes widened and this time it was his turn to tremble.

"Promises, promises," he whispered in her ear.

Catriona's stepmother bit her lip. "Perhaps we should leave them alone."

"No, *they* should leave *us* alone," muttered the older Ellsworth. "I can't have my son causing a scandal on his wedding day. Besides, it's quite ruining my appetite, and I haven't had any wedding cake yet."

"My dear, we can't have *that,*" Rupert said, rising from his chair. "Let us adjourn to our chamber and leave the guests to enjoy their meal without interruption."

"Whatever you say, husband," Catriona said sweetly. As she rose, a gust of wind caught her veil. Rupert caught it and tossed it to a young girl at another table.

The crowd applauded, and Catriona blew them a kiss.

"Enjoy your cake!"

Once in their suite of rooms, Catriona turned to her husband and sighed. "It was a lovely wedding, R-Rupert."

Rupert turned to her with fiery eyes. "Indeed. However, *Catriona mía,* the best is yet to come."

And it was.

About The Author

Susana Ellis has always had stories in her head waiting to come out, especially when she learned to read and her imagination began to soar.

A former teacher, Susana lives in Toledo, Ohio in the summer and Florida in the winter. She is a member of the Central Florida Romance Writers and the Beau Monde chapters of RWA and Maumee Valley Romance Inc.

Website: http://www.SusanaEllis.com
Susana's Parlour (Blog):
https://susanaellisauthor.wordpress.com
Facebook: https://www.facebook.com/Susana.Ellis.5
Twitter: https://twitter.com/SusanaAuthor
Pinterest: http://www.pinterest.com/SusanaAuthor/
Newsletter Sign-Up: http://eepurl.com/u5u3X

Also by Susana Ellis

Treasuring Theresa

She's a country lady. He's a London swell. They have nothing in common. Or have they? Finalist in the 2013 EPIC Awards. *Originally published by Ellora's Cave in their Blush (sweet romance) line.*

Lost and Found Lady

Catalina and Rupert fell in love in Spain in the aftermath of a battle, only to be separated by circumstances. Years later, they find each other again, just as another battle is brewing, but is it too late? *Originally published in* Beaux, Ballrooms, and Battles.

The Third MacPherson Sister

Rebecca's older sisters took the ton by storm while she herself has failed to attract a suitor in four Seasons. Miles is pondering his urgent need for a wife when Rebecca lands in his lap in the nave of Bath Abbey. A match between them seems ordained by the heavens… except for the little matter of his past history with her sisters. *Originally published in* Sweet Summer Kisses.

The Ultimate Escape

Book 1 in The Lady P Chronicles series

On the eve of her wedding, Julia realizes she cannot marry her fiancé after all, no matter that it's been her dream for eight long years. Too distraught to face him, she follows in her mother's footsteps and flees to the future for a brief reprieve.

Oliver knows he has bungled things badly, but he is determined to win the woman he loves, even if he must travel through time to do it.

A Home for Helena

Book 2 in The Lady P Chronicles series

Believing that she has been misplaced in time, Helena Lloyd travels back two hundred years in an attempt to find out where she belongs. Widowed father James Walker has no intention of remarrying until he makes the acquaintance of his daughter's lovely new governess.

Lady Pendleton, a time-traveling Regency lady herself, suspects that these two belong together. First, however, she must help Helena discover her true origins—and hopefully, a home where she belongs. *This is Book 2 of The Lady P Chronicles.*

The Ultimate Escape (Excerpt)

21 November 1812
Pendleton Townhouse
42 Grosvenor Square
London

I always believed my parents' marriage was a love match, although Mama never said so, and Papa wasn't the type to make such emotional declarations, at least not while we were around. He was a gruff man and rarely smiled, but his feelings showed in his eyes by the way they followed her around whenever they were together and how often he touched her hands or shoulder. Nor did I ever see him turn her away when she embraced him or kissed him on the lips, which she was wont to do. And three years ago after he left his earthly shell, my sisters and I thought Mama wouldn't last out the year. She did, though, but she was never truly happy after that. She always seemed to be searching for something to give her life meaning.

But they did have their quarrels. Papa's family were Tories, and Mama, when she found the time, secretly associated with the scandalous Devonshire set. He always pretended not to know, but now that I'm older, I feel pretty certain he did. He knew Mama wasn't the sort of woman to be dictated to, but he couldn't openly condone it either. For the most part, he trusted her to be discreet.

Except that one time. When I was thirteen, they had a dreadful row that went on for days, and then one day, my mother was gone. Papa put it around that she had gone to the country to recover from an illness, but we knew she hadn't. He was beside himself with worry, interrogating us and all over her closest friends, even to the point of calling on the Duchess of Devonshire, Lady Bessborough, Lady Holland, and Lady Melbourne (Mama's Whig friends who, I later discovered, my father detested), in an attempt to discover her whereabouts. All to no avail. Finally, he just shut himself up in his study and refused to allow anyone inside except servants and numerous bottles of spirits.

A fortnight later, Mama returned and hugged us all, promising she would never leave us again, and she and Papa went upstairs to their rooms and resolved their differences. They were happier after that, but neither could be induced to tell us anything about their quarrel or where she had been during that time.

It wasn't until two years later that I discovered her journal and learned the truth, shocking and unbelievable though it is. During those two weeks, Mama wrote that she had escaped two hundred years into the future to the twentieth century!

When confronted with the journal, she admitted it was true. Apparently, the newly-married William Wilberforce had acquainted Papa with the facts about Mama's dealings with the immoral Devonshire set—nearly all of whom had children by other men than their husbands—and told him he'd best get his household in order before he, too, became a laughingstock. Papa had been so humiliated that he'd come home in a fit of temper and demanded that Mama cease all of her political activities and content herself with her role as wife and mother. When she refused—and he had to know she would—he threatened to banish her to the country until she agreed.

They quarreled for several days, and then one day she walked off and didn't come back. In her diary, she wrote that she had found herself in an odd little shop on Gracechurch Street where a gypsy lady told fortunes and such. Mama confided in her, saying that she didn't want to face anyone she knew until she had had a chance to consider her options and resolve what to do about her marriage.. The gypsy, who goes by the name of Madame Herne, offered to send her away into the future for a time, and Mama was desperate enough to accept, after being reassured that she could return when she wished to.

She never would tell me what happened during those two weeks, and she burned the journal after I confronted her with it so that nobody else would read it. Nor do I know what she told Papa. But he never questioned her behavior again, and I believe their marriage was stronger afterward. She had a locked drawer in her desk that she only opened when she was alone, and when we were ill she used to bring us smooth white pellets instead of the usual willow bark tea, and she adamantly refused to allow us to be bled for any reason. I once caught a glimpse of her in some scandalous nightrail that made Papa's eyes light up when he saw her in it, and she later confessed that she had got it from some shop in the future called "Victoria's Secret."

She didn't leave us again until after Papa's death, and before she did, she made sure to tell my sisters and me beforehand. Philippa and Sarah didn't believe her at first, and I think they are still a bit skeptical and disapproving, but they are both happily married society matrons now and can't imagine why anyone would want to travel in time. I, on the other hand, have always been fascinated by the idea.

And now, on the eve of my marriage, I find myself longing to escape, at least until I can reflect clearly on my future. If I do not appear at St. George's tomorrow, my future with Oliver will certainly be ended. But after what I overheard this evening, I comprehend that I cannot marry a man who only wants me to be a mother to his child, who likely still loves his deceased wife, my one-time best friend. Not even though I've loved him desperately my entire life and he may be my only chance of escaping spinsterhood.

The house is asleep, so I change into a traveling gown and pelisse, scoop up my jewelry and a stash of coins into a reticule, and hail a hackney to take me to Gracechurch Street. A bold move, but then, I am my mother's daughter. And I'd sooner brave the unknown than the consequences of leaving my betrothed at the altar.

Made in the USA
Middletown, DE
03 November 2019

77806697R00066